Praise for Troul
Br

Of 'Whal

'A great setting. A great sense of place. Masterful – I loved it!'

-ChipLit Prize-winning story, judge Nicholas Royle (author, Reader of Creative Writing at Manchester Writing School, editor of Salt publishing)

[W + (D-d)] x TQ/MxNa' excellent and daring, citing it as an example of how style can describe and inform more than any passage of exposition.

-Adam Craig, editor at Cinnamon Press

'…a short story perfectly in tune with itself… Calm, confident and disturbing: a treat to read and re-read' –

-Maria Donovan, in her adjudication of the PENfro prize.

Thought provoking and intriguing, Powell's stories make you think and relate to a world we are all far too familiar with. You feel deeply for her characters

-Emma Jane Mackay

Trouble Crossing The Bridge

Diana Powell

Trouble Crossing the Bridge
A short story collection by
Diana Powell

First published in Ireland in 2020 by Chaffinch Press

ISBN : 978-1-9161545-4-4

For Noah and Ffion

Contents

Risk Factor

Black Friday.

S – (T x V) + E = C.

(where S = savings on purchase; T = time spent in line; V = the value of your time (e.g. your hourly wage); E = enjoyment factor; C = true cost.

But none of this calculates the risk factor.

S… (Savings on purchase.)

Scarlet.

So bright her eyes break into Picasso jags. Once upon a time, she had seen a Picasso, in a gallery in Paris. But that was long ago, or happened to somebody else.

'Bright colours are for the trash hustling on Fifth,' Henry told her.

'When did you ever drive down Fifth?' she wanted to ask.

'My husband passed in April,' she tells Nancy, whose name and smile are pinned to her front for all to see.

Nancy makes all those moues and tics she has grown used to; ushers coats the colour of dirge in front of her.

'This one, I think.'

A coat. Red. Cashmere. She slips her hand beneath the see-through protective wrapper, touches the surface. 'Yes,' it says. She digs deeper, catches a shimmer of lining.

'Satin is for whores.'

'How do you know, Henry?' she never said.

The figures on the price label are for a small, once-used car.

'I could take a couple of hundred off, maybe,' Nancy tells her.

'No, no need.'

Back home, she unwraps it from the bag, the box, the tissue, the bows and spreads it on the bed, and stares for a while. Then she nudges it across, to where Henry lay once a month, on a Saturday night, for their 'concourse'.

She shimmies beside it, and runs her fingers along the 'underfleece of Hircus goat kids'.

Is Hircus a breed? Or a place? Where? The other side of the world, perhaps. Somewhere not here; somewhere imagined, on those monthly Saturdays, staring at the ceiling. The coat has been 'imagined' for her, according to the booklet; imagined by two handsome French men, with smiles as big as Nancy's. The nap parts with the slick of her fingers, and she puts her lips to it, scarlet to scarlet.

'Only whores wear make-up,' Henry said. But Henry isn't here.

Her tongue lingers over it. The give beneath her fingertips eases her, somehow. A loosening inside.

'Your first time, I'm guessing,' Nora says to her. Nora is standing next to her in the 'Line'. 'Nora' is a blah, blah, blah coming at her, from a tunnel of racoon fur. 'Nora' is all she's heard, until now.

Nora doesn't know about the goats, how they roam the plains of Inner Mongolia at minus forty degrees. She stands there, cocooned in nylon Michelin-Man hoops, stuffed with cotton-candy, topped with that rim of racoon. She can't imagine the natural moulting of the goats in springtime, aided by a fine toothcomb and the gentlest of strokes. She doesn't see Batu crooning to them, as he combs their silken locks, and gathers it in organic sacks, ready for the two Frenchmen to take it away.

For her, bulk is everything, all that is needed to keep the cold at bay.

'You'll learn,' she thinks Nora's thinking. 'You'll learn to wear something warmer than a thin wool coat (fifty per cent acrylic, most like, after all.)'

The racoon comes closer. 'I'm after a TV. 90 per cent reduction, according to the ad. Is that what you're here for?'

Racoons and Hircus kids don't go together. Yet here they

are, in the parking-lot of a mall on Thanksgiving night. But she's got a TV, bought in the summer, taking up half the wall.

'Television is for the illiterate,' Henry said.

The 'literate' sat, staring at a still point in front of a sparse room. They listened to silence.

Now, she likes the soaps, the daytime talk-shows. Now, she hears noise all the time, because the TV is on all the time. And a radio in the kitchen, and another TV in the bedroom. An eternal hum in her head. A hummmm that sometimes gets straightened into words.

Black. Friday. Shopping. Mall.

'Thanksgiving night,' said Lorrie-Mae, her favourite news-anchor. Lorrie-Mae, so pretty, so blonde.

'Blondes are…'

'Yes, I know, Henry.'

She told the girl in the salon she wanted her hair the same shade as Lorrie-Mae's. 'You know her?' It was the summer; she wanted to match the sun.

'I'm not too old?' she asked. Nancy? Nora? Nell? Nell, perhaps.

'You are never too old, madam!'

Now, it's the Fall, and Lorrie-Mae has told her about a shopping experience she'd never known existed before.

She's done 'shop-till-you-drop', all-day-sprees, week-long binges, personal-shoppers (what's the point in that?).

Black Friday… something new. A way to spend Thanksgiving night, when there's no husband, family or friends, to visit, or visiting. They even have a formula for it, to explain how it works.

It seemed the perfect thing.

'Jewellery,' she tells Nora.

Shining facets of diamond wink at her from a velvet cushioned box, hidden beneath her bed. Sinuous threads of gold sidle towards her, run through her hands.

Better to pick something different from Nora, better not to be rivals for the same purchase.

Here, it will be big, brash, glitzy. Fake. The kind worn by the tarts on Fifth.

'Yeh, I saw that in the ads, too. Good reductions, I read.'

'My husband passed in May,' she says.

She waits for the Aw and the pity to fumble from the racoon's mouth.

Instead, there's a hush in the Line, followed by a vague susurration. Nora turns away, steadies herself. Ready, steady…

She does the same, feeling the rise within her. Feeling herself stretch, as air rises from her lungs, gasps between her lips. And…breathe.

'Breathe!' she tells Hector Aspen, watching on the news next morning. Lorrie-Mae is telling her all about him, whilst the screen shows video footage, taken by a passer-by. Hector was in another Mall, across town. Hector didn't save anything in the sale, because he wasn't shopping. He was a security guard, already on the inside of the store. Should have been retired, but wanted the extra money. Too old to have a wall of people surge down on him, push him to the floor, knocking the breath out of him.

'You need to swallow it back down,' she tells him. 'The other way from me. Take it back in, then out again.'

'Breathe,' she told Henry, when she found him lying on the garage floor.

'Breathe,' she told herself. 'Do something.'

She got down beside him.

'Henry?'

T… (Time spent in line.)

This time, she's given in to nylon and polyester… a sleeping-bag. An extra layer to shroud the Hircus kids, not organic cotton, now. The Frenchmen won't be pleased. But she'd got here the night before, so has longer to wait. 'Better chance of the best deals,' the magazine had told her. 'Better chance of the best deals,' Nettie tells her, 'look how far up the Line we are; how close we are to the doors!'

She's brought a flask, and some food, and has a money-pouch strapped round her waist beneath her coat. She read all these things in the same article.

'My husband passed last year.'

'Aw. Never mind. This'll be worth it. You'll see. Whatever you're after.'

The Booker family weren't even in the Line. They hadn't got that far, the news report said the next day. They only made it to the parking lot, where there was just one space left. One space, two cars. The women got out, started yelling. Then the men.

'It is not known who started the shooting.' Two dead husbands. They showed a picture of one of the wives kneeling on the floor beside him, crying.

'Henry?'

She supposed she should be doing something.

There was a number she should call.

There was something you could do. Hands on the chest, press down. Henry didn't like to be touched. He preferred her to lie still, while he did what he must do.

She guessed the tarts on Fifth did a lot of touching.

She supposed she should be crying.

V… (The value of your time.)

'I've taken time off work for this. I shouldn't have – haven't got many days left, but I reckon it will be worth it. I've worked it out. See!'

Neeta pulls a scrap of paper from her pocket.

Hourly wage =

Number of hours =

Price of computer =

'If it's the price they say it is, I'll be a hundred dollars up, so yes, it's worth it. How about you? How much do you earn?'

'Oh, I don't… I'm a widow… two years gone… I…'

There is so much money. All the shopping she has done, and there is still so much money. The savings Henry had made… Well, they never took vacations, did they? And they never ate out. And he never bought her anything, did he? Or for himself, if she was being fair.

His pension. Such a wonderful pension! So safe! But a just reward for all his hard work, the company told her.

'What have you been doing today?/What the fuck have you been doing while I'm earning my butt off?/Do you do anything but sit here on your fat butt, day in, day out?/Look at you, you can't even keep yourself looking good for me, when I come home. You worthless bitch!'

It was only when he drank too much, the week after their 'concourse' usually. The week when he always came home late.

Now, she likes to think she is contributing to the economy, society. Shopping, spending is necessary for the capitalist system to work, she has heard on the news.

But she won't tell Neeta that.

Next morning, half way across the state, the Morgan family crashed their car, with the two parents killed outright.

'It is believed that Mr Morgan couldn't see out the back window, on account of all their purchases squashed into the back seat, along with their two girls,' Lorrie-Mae told her.

'And the girls were squealing and shouting about their cool bargains, so were distracting their father,' Lorrie didn't add.

He made a bad judgement in a lane move, and wham! A truck went into them. A giant, latest model TV survived unscathed.

Henry was unscathed. She thought there should be blood. He had hit his head, hadn't he, when he fell? Hit it on the corner of the concrete step, the paramedics said, the autopsy said. But she couldn't see any blood. Did it matter, anyway? It was the heart-attack that killed him.

'If we'd have got there sooner, ma'am. Maybe…'

But she was in shock, she was panicking, wasn't she?

He turned his head and looked at her, his lips mouthing… something.

'For god's sake, woman, can't you do anything right?/ What's the matter with you?/You are so fucking useless./ You couldn't even do that simple thing, to save your life.'

'Your life,' she mouthed back.

'What is it, Henry?' She put her face closer. She noticed his lips were blue.

E… (Enjoyment factor.)

'I read it in a magazine, in the hairdressers. This formula…'

'Oh, yes, I've read that, too. If I remember…'

'The thing is – we're supposed to be enjoying it. It's not just about the savings. That's what the guy said. It's gotta be, like, watching a movie, costing, say, twelve dollars. Said something about 'adrenaline', too. 'Do you get the same thrill for bagging a bargain, as going to an amusement park, which may set you back sixty dollars or more?'

'Well,' I thought, 'yes, I do'. And you, do you enjoy all this?'

Yes, even though it's her third year, now. Even though her neighbour is always the same, give or take the origin of the fur. Fox, this time, she guesses. Even though the stroke of her fingers down the Hircus hair is as familiar to her, now, as her own skin. Even though the saving is nothing to her, with all the money she still has, somehow.

And, in truth, she's never been to an amusement park,

on any of those rides that are supposed to make you scream with a strange mixture of fear and joy.

And when she last went to watch a movie, it cost no more than a couple of dollars, and she's not really sure that that was her. It was so long ago.

But 'yes' she tells Noreen. 'Of course I do. That moment when the Line grows quiet, when we get ready to run… that's the biggest buzz of all.'

For Aaron Hadley, the biggest buzz was when he reached an item just ahead of another guy. When he put his hands on it, eyeballed his opponent, and said, 'Bea-cha! Got it! Hard luck, bro!'

Only this time, the other guy didn't want to give up on the camera he was holding, and he was bigger than him.

'An altercation followed in which Mr Hadley fell to the floor. It is still unclear where the knife came from or who wielded it. People were screaming, running away from the body.'

After a while, she got up and went back into the house. There was no point in staying beside Henry any longer. He was surely dead, no two ways about it. She guessed she should make that phone call now, but there was something so… peaceful about the place, different from the usual silence. Perhaps that's what they meant by a 'deathly hush'. She sat down, and picked up Henry's paper, the one she was never allowed to read. She licked a finger to turn the pages, creasing them as she went, ripping off a corner, then crumpled the whole affair, and tossed it in the bin. A quiver of a nerve deep inside, or the tic of a muscle? Was this what the beginnings of joy felt like?

C… (True Cost.)

She's glad Nora's with her, now. Or Nettie, Neeta, Noreen or whoever – she's never really been sure of the names. They can't really have all began with 'N', can they?

They ran together into the changing-rooms, when the first shots were heard.

'There are always fatalities on Black Friday,' she tells her companion. 'But there's never been a mass shooting before. We're the first!'

Nora's eyes narrow, and shift towards her. She's pushed the racoon hood back. It's the first time she's ever seen a face.

The sound of gunfire comes closer.

She hopes it's Lorrie-Mae who tells it on the news. Tells how a man who thought he would get a smart-phone for fifty bucks got angry when the sales guy said it was a hundred-fifty 'you must have heard wrong', and drew out a semi-automatic. He killed five people, including two women who were hiding in a changing-booth. They were holding hands.

Young goats are playing together on the plains of the Mongolian desert. The sun is shining. Springtime again. The handsome Frenchmen stand beside Batu, nodding, handing over the money. A handsome Frenchman had approached her when she was looking at the Picassos in Paris. It was spring, then, too; the blossom on the trees, the dancing Seine. 'What do you think of them?' he asked. 'All those funny angles! They make my eyes go funny!' she replied. He bought her a coffee. They talked for a while, then went back to her hotel. The happiest moments of her life. He asked her to stay, but she thought it was too risky. She came home, and married her high-school sweetheart. Henry.

She's glad she's wearing the cashmere coat. Well, she always does for Black Friday. Red. Scarlet. Blood-coloured. The blood doesn't show too much as it spreads across her stomach, whereas Nora's green parka looks like a camo-jacket. She takes Nora's hand.

S – (T x V) + E = C.

'Look at it this way: if the number you get in 'C' is

positive, then all that queuing is worth it. Even if you've got to stand there for hours, in the cold and wet. Snow, even.

But if the number is low, negative you could say, you would be better off staying at home.

And another thing. You may do all that queuing, and then the item you wanted is sold out, or not at the price you expected. Or… you get pneumonia from all that waiting (it has happened!) and then you have to miss work for weeks, and pay your hospital bills, and so anything you saved is lost. Or you could be one of those victims of Black Friday injuries, or even fatalities. You might be surprised by the statistics!

So remember – none of this calculates the risk factor.'

Crying at Three Minutes To…

Tick-tock. Tick-tock.

June, 1947. That's when it all began. The Countdown to Zero, Armageddon. The Doomsday Clock, set at seven minutes to midnight. Or… no more than an orange, white and black magazine cover, with the time chosen because it looked good to the eye.

11:53 p.m., June 14th, 1947. Birth. I don't remember it, though some do, I've heard – telling of a rhythmic blip, blip, blip that must be their mother's heartbeat. 'Then there's a bright light, a rush of noise, a figure waiting,' they insist. Not too different from a near-death experience, when you think about it, except the welcoming silhouette's a midwife, not God. And what about the pain, the pulling and pushing and twisting of head and limb? And no going back, however much you want to.

According to the scientists, it's all nonsense – something to do with a new-born's hippocampus not being fully developed. But what do they know about it, about anything? What do they know about me?

11:53 p.m. That's seven minutes to midnight. The clock on the hospital wall would have been one of those simple, round, analog affairs, with bold hands, easy for all to see.

Like the Doomsday Clock, with its firm, black hour hand, pointing straight up, and the dubious, white, tapered minute hand, hesitating between the seven and eight, (depending on who you ask), and big white dots standing in for numbers. Four dots, because it's not the whole clock, just the final quarter, perfect for a rectangular page.

I'm not sure if my mother noticed the ward clock, or only the nurse, eager to record the time of my arrival, along with my name 'Nathaniel Thomas Fischer', 'Nate' for ever more. And I don't know if the middle of the night is a good time to come into the world. Bad, I guess – tired midwife, tired doctor. Tired mother. That's what she told me, years later. 'I'd already had enough by then', meaning the six kids she'd had before me, the two husbands, the two jobs she was juggling all hours. The thirty dollars plus a day.

Blah, blah. Etc, etc. 'Sorry, and all that,' she said.

Perhaps that flaccid hippocampus isn't such a bad deal, especially since it stops you remembering your early years as well (except, I'll bet, for those nerds who remember their births). 'Infantile amnesia', it's called. Isn't it better that way?

Better not to remember that my life started off crap, with a mother who didn't want me, and a father (or one of the likely candidates, leastways) who disappeared, and the boyfriends who came and went and beat me when they were there.

And what I do remember, I reckoned was just life, same for everyone. I never thought how tough it was for me, how close I came to dying. That time Crew, the latest guy, dropped me down the trailer steps – 1949, when the Russkies tested their first atomic bomb. Or when my mom left all us kids alone in the trailer, and Laney, the eldest, fell asleep with her cigarette burning. 1953 that was, when I was six years old. Yes, we all nearly died. Well, so did the rest of the world, since the U.S. and the Soviet Union each tested their first thermonuclear weapons within six months of each other. Hydrogen bombs, making Little Boy, with its sixty-four kilos of uranium to drop on Hiroshima look like a pop-gun pellet.

Uranium. U. Atomic number 92. 'Uranium-235 has the distinction of being the only naturally occurring fissile isotope.' Whoopee for Uranium.

U. A 'U'. That was the first choice for the 'Bulletin' cover (that's Bulletin of the Atomic Scientists, to be precise). Because U was the shit that made it all happen; well, U and the scientists who'd developed it. What if they'd stayed with the 'U'? Would anyone pay so much attention? There'd be no hands to move, when they were debating the status of the world's security. What could they do instead? Doodle on the U? Turn it upside down? Sideways?

No, a clock has so much more impact, an image able to transcend a paper magazine cover. An icon for our nuclear times, capable of being adjusted to suit Armageddon's proximity. That's what they say.

Not that me and the rest of John Q. Public had heard about it in the beginning, or even for a couple of decades down the line. No Internet back then, no twenty-four/seven TV; not that many TVs, truth be told, especially in trailer parks. Same way most of us had no idea how perilous things were. Didn't know about that '49 bomb, when they moved the minute hand for the first time; or about those hydrogen explosions in '53 – the closest the Clock's ever been to midnight. Perhaps it was all just another form of infantile amnesia, only collective, not individual. Or 'dissociation', perhaps. Something the shrinks have told me I suffer from, amongst other disorders. 'The suppression of 'early life' trauma, a defensive mechanism humans employ. Whereas, really, it can be beneficial for it all to be out in the open.'

I don't agree with that. No matter what they say, I'm sure it's better not to know, and keep such stuff buried deep down. I never wanted to know that my mother didn't want me, or about the bruises, the bleeding and the burns. Just like I wish I'd never found out I shared my birthday with the Doomsday Clock.

1963. Twelve minutes to midnight. It's a funny one, that. An anomaly for the Clock, an anomaly for me, when the hand was moved to the safe side of the ten for the first time, something that hadn't happened before, and hasn't happened much since. And yet 'What about the Cuban Missile Crisis?' everyone asks. 'The closest we got/the nearest to the brink'. Etc, etc. And yet, look what they did. + 5. Any 'plus' is good, but plus five is about as good as it's ever been. So what's the answer?

That's when they like to point out the Clock doesn't get set in real time. Instead, their Board meets twice a year to deliberate the situation. And in 1963 the Partial Test Ban Treaty got signed, limiting atmospheric testing, slowing the arms race – hooray! Oh, and by the way, they didn't really know what the hell was going on; everything happened so quickly – crisis, climax and resolution within thirteen days – that they didn't have a chance to reset the Clock. Well, fair enough, since it's said now that even the policy makers didn't really have a clue, that Kennedy and Khrushchev were damned lucky – not to mention the rest of us, who didn't know the score, either, didn't know how close we came to being blown to smithereens, kingdom come, wherever you fancy.

So that's how what should have been a bad year turned out to be pretty damn good, (Kennedy's assassination apparently doesn't count, being more of a personal kind of occurrence) and it was the same for sixteen-year old me. Sixteen – I'd left home the year before, couldn't stand the beatings any more, and was living on the streets, surrounded by junkies, no-accounts, and screw-balls. Not to mention the plain mother-killers. Well, I hadn't quite reached junkie status myself, was still happy smoking weed back then – my new form of memory suppression, much more effective than that infantile amnesia, far more mind-numbing than the Board's 'lack of information'. But then I got picked up by some homeless charity, got placed in a decent foster home, got myself cleaned up (relatively), and even found myself doing okay in school. Suddenly, I was doing better than any time since I'd been born. Same as the Clock.

I'm skipping to 1984, now. It's not that zilch happened in between. It's twenty years after all. There were some bad years – '68, when I'd come of age, supposed to be a man, when the drugs took hold – though some said that was good, cos it got me out of 'Nam. Turned myself around again, and got hitched in 1972; things were pretty good then. Some things, like those, stand out. It's the same with the Clock. It's something you have to remember about it – they don't move the hands all the time. Only twenty times, in the last sixty-five years. I guess it would lose its impact, if they were moving it every tiny security glitch, guess it would become boring, and no-one would pay attention. It's the same with a life.

But then came 1984, well, it would be, wouldn't it? George Orwell and all that. The dangers of communism… or was it Fascism? Or was that 'Animal Farm'? The Russians were certainly in there somewhere. Afghanistan, to be precise. They'd been there for a while, sparking the American boycott of the Olympic Games in 1980, causing their retaliation in the LA games in '84. But that was nothing compared to what was going on in the arms race, with Reagan deploying Pershing II ballistic and cruise missiles to Western Europe, in a push to win the Cold War.

And that's when I found out about it, the year I discovered the existence of the Clock, lying in a hospital bed, after a car crash that was my own fault. Drink, stronger drugs (my own personal A-bombs), thoughts elsewhere… thoughts on my broken marriage, my kids taken away from me, my lost job, lost because of the drink, drugs, broken marriage. Chicken and egg, egg and chicken. I blamed her, she blamed me, I blamed etc. Tick-tock, tick-tock.

So there I am, unable to move, for weeks, going into months, and there's the TV in front of me, which I can just about half watch with my one un-bandaged eye. And then, this documentary comes on about it, about the Doomsday Clock, that I'd never heard of before, even though it began the day I was born. So I learnt about how it all started with the Bulletin of Atomic Scientists, and the decision to move the minute hand was taken by their board of directors in consultation with its board of Sponsors, including sixteen

Nobel laureates.

'There isn't a real, physical clock,' I said to the nurse who came in to check my temperature. 'A lot of people think there is – that it's there, in a room in the University of Chicago. But actually it's a metaphor, a symbol of the countdown to global catastrophe.'

She didn't know what I was talking about.

'That's the problem. Too few people do. We're all walking blindfold to Doomsday. You don't know how close to midnight we are. Three minutes! Three minutes right now – practically the worst it's ever been! The Cold War is freezing! Reagan's not talking. Seriously, Armageddon's coming now.'

She made that same little tsking noise, like when I wouldn't eat my food, then click-clipped from the room. The shrink appeared a few moments later.

'That's the problem,' I told him, too. 'Anybody who says anything about it gets labelled crazy. These guys are scientists – some of the best in the world. You're a scientist. Surely you get what they're saying. Something's got to be done about it!'

The guy kept on scribbling in his file. He's still writing on it now – or another of his kind; well, a woman, as it happens (a sign of progress in one direction, at least). Page after page after page.

When I came out, I walked the streets, wearing a sandwich board with the words 'The end of the world is nigh' written on it. It seemed the right thing to do. I was on the streets again, anyway. Mia wouldn't take me back, wouldn't let me see the kids. It didn't help that I kept on turning up at the door, wearing my sign. But I felt it was my duty. Now that I knew what was happening out there, I felt it was my duty to share. That was what the Board wanted. 1) To get smart about what the world was facing. 2) To share that knowledge. 3) Campaign to your government – I was working on that.

'I'm not one of those people, okay?' I told her. 'One of

those prophets of doom, apocalypse merchants. It's not as if I'm David Berg, with his Kohoutek comet, or Jim Jones with his nuclear visions. This is based on scientific fact! The Clock doesn't predict the future. It simply reacts to whatever shit we're in. If you read the Bulletin…' I waved the latest copy in front of her face. I'd started subscribing.

She shut the door in my face.

The sandwich board was useful, sometimes, for sheltering from the rain.

Well, it didn't happen, though it came pretty close. The world didn't end, and neither did I. It was a miracle for both of us. Who would have thought that only a few years later, they'd be moving the hand to seventeen minutes to midnight, the furthest it had been since it began? So far away that the original design hadn't allowed for it. 11:43 p.m. was off the page! But I guess they didn't mind, I guess they were thrilled about it. The Soviet Union was breaking apart, it was the end of the Cold War. Together with the U.S., the START 1 treaty was signed. This was it now. Everything would be on the up from there, except for the hands of the Clock! And yes, I was happy, too; happy for the world, happy for myself. I'd turned myself around again, quit the human-billboard scene, ditched the Apocalypse prophesying. Okay, I kept up my daily correspondence with the Government, but wasn't that what the Bulletin advocated?

I had a new relationship, a girl called Sylvie, where everything seemed to be going well. Was allowed to see the children, and getting on with my ex, and a new job, which was going well, too. Yeah, forty-four years old, and everything neat. You could say it was the best year of my life, better than '63, even. Just like the Clock. Again.

And that's when it clicked. There was an article in the paper about the Board and its purpose – well, that was good; they should celebrate, as well as scare. And this time, they printed a graph of the Clock's adjustments, matching the minutes to the years. And that's when I saw the pattern.

'Do you know?' I said to Sylvie. 'I've never seen it before…'

I'd told her I shared my birthday with the Clock. It was something I told everyone, before going on to explain about it. I still believed it was my obligation to educate, but without the sandwich board.

'I mean… look at this. Worst time of my life, worst time on the Clock. Best time, best time on the Clock. The pattern of my life is following the Clock, which is following the world. It's all so obvious. See!'

She looked at the page, looked at my face, and shook her head.

I started digging down into my memory, wanting now to recollect what I had chosen to forget, checking facts, where I could, for all the skipped years. I even got in touch with my mom and siblings (those who were left), to see what they could tell me. And everything I found proved my theory. Me and the Clock marched in time, ticked the minutes off together, you could say.

Okay, so I got a bit obsessed with it; Sylvie packed her bags soon after, muttering something about 'getting help'. Or 'saphead'. But, really, I didn't care, because there was nothing I could do about it. Whatever happened in the world, however much they moved the hands of the Clock, well, that was the deck I got dealt in life.

Sometimes I find myself wondering if it's all down to the original design. If they'd stuck with the U, would my life have been different? You can't synch with a U, can you? It's just down, round and up. Not back and fore, according to the move of a minute hand, according to a gang of scientists sitting in a room around an imaginary clock.

All I could do was keep an eye on it, I supposed. Watch the news, buy the Bulletin, check the Clock, and just hope that midnight wouldn't strike, that Armageddon wouldn't arrive. And of course, if it did, I'd be dead, anyway, along with most of the world. So, come to think of it, did any of it matter at all?

It got easier in 2010, the year it went on line. I could check it every day. Not that it changed, of course; not for months. But still, there was something comforting in feeling so connected to it.

I – along with anyone else who tuned in (not sure of the numbers there!) – was able to watch the hand put back by one minute live. One of the occasions when they dragged out a real clock, for demonstration purposes, scrapping the symbolic/metaphor idea in the interests of visual effect. They did the same thing in the lectures they held, painting a map of the world on the clock-face, to remind you what it was all about.

It was just chance, perhaps, that the first online adjustment was the one little 'plus' in all those years, since the '91 peak. Didn't last long. After that, it was back down, down, down, all the way, except for a few spells of levelling out. And, of course, it had been the same with my life.

2007 had been a real bad year, with the Clock going down to a five. That was the year climate change got added to the danger list, along with the usual nuclear threat (as if that on its own wasn't enough, with North Korea testing a nuke, Iran getting interested in the whole shebang, the inadequate security of nuclear materials. Twenty-six thousand nuclear weapons in the U.S. and Russia! 'We are at the brink of a second nuclear age!' the Board cried.)

There were other new 'risk probability factors', too. It wasn't only uranium and plutonium that weren't being looked after carefully enough. There was the possible escape of highly lethal pathogens. And the killer robot problem. 'The Terminator come true!'

Still, the Clock got an update from a Famous Graphic Designer, who made sure to heap praise on the original, in the process. Before that, it hadn't changed much in all those years, except for different colours for the background, and, one year, both hands were white – I've no idea why.

Personally, I've never thought much of the new version – just black on white, thicker lines, bolder, like a child's drawing. But the Board was happy enough, and adopted the Clock as their official identity. A logo. An icon. Well, it always had been, hadn't it?

That was the year I started coughing from the emissions in the shithole I was working in. (Climate).

That was the year I got diagnosed. (Disease). Well, I should have known. All that bad living, all those pathogens loose about the place. At least I hadn't spotted any killer robots around. But who knew what was happening with AI behind the scenes?

2013. The designer of the first Clock died that year – before the Clock stopped, and the world with it. Still, she made it to ninety-six, which can't be bad for someone living in such desperate times.

And the press coverage of her death got me going over it all, over and over again. Not that it had ever left me, with checking the time daily, and my campaigning, and Internet trawling. But, still, I went back to the very beginning – mine and the Clock's. Birth. Day one. Seven minutes to… 'Tick-tock. Tick-tock. Tock-tick. Tock-tick.' And that's when I got it, I understood what had to be done.

November 14th of that same year. The 5th Doomsday Clock Symposium. I shouldn't have gone. Their brief was 'Communicating Catastrophe', but they wouldn't communicate with me. I got carried from the hall by the security guys. Not that you see it on the live feed – they cut it somehow, even though it was supposed to be 'live'. How did they do that, I've been trying to figure? But then, they're scientists. It's the kind of thing they'd know, along with nuclear fission, carbon emissions, bio-deficients. How to make a bomb. But when it came to the 'Personalization of Catastrophe', they didn't have a clue. They should have been putting me up on the podium, not dragging me away. You couldn't get a better illustration of 'personalization' than me – wasn't I a living example of it all?

All I'd wanted to do was make them understand.

'How do we prevent catastrophe?' they asked.

'Fix me!' I shouted from the front row.

'How do we move the clock hands backwards?'

'Look after me, make me better. It's as simple as that.'

Okay, perhaps I'd got a bit worked up, raised my voice a little too much, waved my hands around – which may, or may not, have come up against some other person's face (though that was negotiable). But still, they should have listened. There they were, going on about the 'destruction of the human psyche', saying it was the responsibility of health professionals to pay attention, and yes, I heard them saying 'that guy needs help', yet what did they do? Just had me bounced out of there.

Soon after that I knew just how sick I was.

2016.

In and out, in and out. The Four Horsemen are racing through my mind, along with Frankenstein robots, and mushroom clouds, and a plague of locusts.

'Here,' the nurse says, 'another shot will make you sleep, will make them go away.'

But it doesn't. And now Zachariae Isstrom is crashing all around me, rising over my head.

'Do you know about Zachariae Isstrom?' I ask the nurse. 'A huge Greenland glacier that broke loose in 2012, carrying enough water to raise the seas by eighteen inches.'

'Do you know that there are sixteen thousand, three hundred nuclear weapons in the world?'

'Do you know about Ebola and all the other zoonotic diseases?' (Of course, she does, she's a nurse!)

Tick, tick, Chomsky says. There's no tock for him; just the world and life ticking away. Like it is for me.

It's my zero hour, my cry at midnight, my apocalypse now. They don't word it that way. But saying 'there's nothing more we can do,' is just about the same. Or 'all we can do is keep you comfortable.'

So I'm lying here, piped into tubes, plugged into wires, monitored by a screen, that pulses flashing figures, plus and minuses, lines as up and down as a Himalayan range. Just like the Doomsday Dashboard, with its graphs, bar and pi charts, notched by figures and percentage analyses. Only, on there, it's about quantities of nuclear weapons, their storage, their security; bio-threats, cyber conflict; sea-level rise, arctic sea melt, atmospheric carbon dioxide. Temperature. For it, for me. Up, up, up, no matter what they do.

And, sure enough, there's the Clock, my own personal version, on the top left of the screen. Clocks are different now. How many people even have them these days? Yes, you still see them on public buildings. But there's no big round face on the wall of the ward, any more. So different from the day I was born. So different from the one that sat on the wall in that room in the University of Chicago – or would, if it had ever existed (it's still real hard to pin that one down). But, look, it's mainly digital now. Tiny white numbers for the nurse to check constantly, because times are important in the business of illness, too. The exact hour/minute/second of every procedure must always be recorded – when drugs are given, when a test is done, when a doctor visits, when the vital signs change. Yes, my own little Doomsday Clock. They don't realise I've always had one. I keep on telling them, but they don't listen. They won't believe that I don't need this computerised time function to tell me where I'm at.

'Three minutes to midnight!' I say to the doctor. 'Eleven fifty-seven! It's bad, but there's still time. You've just got to do more. Keeping me comfortable is not enough!'

And all they do is pop me another pill, or slide in another

needle. Anything to shut me up…

Another (legal) memory suppressant, another thought blocker, another snap in my synapses – it's what drugs do to you. I learnt it long ago. A faulty connection in my brain. And then it's MRIs, x-rays, BT/BP/HR/RR checks. All saying 'You don't have long!'

'It's not just me you have to worry about, it's you. Don't you understand?' I tell them, just like I told the Bulletin scientists at the Symposium. But all they do is call in the shrink; or the Priest, if he's around, who tells me I'll have reached my three score and ten next year, and really, that's all the Good Book allows us, so shouldn't I be glad? Hallelujah!

Sometimes I think the shrink is beginning to be worried, that I'm getting to her. After all, she is supposed to listen sympathetically, she is supposed to believe me. And yes, sometimes, it's like she's wondering what if I'm telling the truth. That I'm right about the Clock and me, how we've always been together, how we've always matched.

'So if I die, midnight will strike and the world will end. You have to do everything in your power to keep me alive, to keep the world alive!'

And I see her pen hesitate over my file, and her eyes shift over to my vital signs, but that's not enough. She needs to tell the doctors in charge. The top guys in the land, in the world. She needs to get them to help me.

'If you could keep me going until a hundred, well, I'd be happy with that. The Priest and his seventy years – we're way beyond that, now. Think how many centenarians there are.' And really, the planet shouldn't complain if it gets that far – well, mankind shouldn't anyway, considering all the shit it's put out there. In fact, it should count itself lucky to have survived that long.

And yes, there'd be something fitting in the Clock striking midnight a hundred years since it/I was born. It's not so unlikely, considering they're calling 2047 the year of climate departure. Another predicted 'end of the world'.

Temperatures off the scale. Cities washed away. Mass extinction.

So let's go out together then. The world, the Clock, and me. When we've all had our day.

But not yet. It's too soon, too soon. Help me, help us. Lower my blood pressure. Slow my heart rate. Reduce my temperature. Ease my tortured brain. Turn back the hands of time. NOW!

Please.

Tick-tock; tick-tock. Tick…

Herr Munch visits the Zoo

Tiger chases him down the street. Death and sinew, wrapped in fur. Together, they weave in and out of the serried lime trees. From the branches, the monkeys throw peanuts at him, while parakeets screech and whistle. Then ragamuffin Bear lumbers around the corner, ahead of him. He is trapped, he stumbles. Two giant shadows rear above his fallen body. Tiger offers him a splayed fan of daggers. Which one shall finish him? Now, all the other animals – sea lions, goats, zebra, even the gentle deer – gather around, baying and gibing, at Pig's command. The sharpest blade is chosen, and etches a fine line beneath his heart. Behind, in the window of the last house, he sees the woman watching. 'Help me,' he cries. She smiles and turns away.

He opened his eyes to an Angel hovering above him, in a shaft of white light.

'Wake up, Herr Munch, you've been dreaming! Too much excitement yesterday, perhaps. Hushed, now, we do not want your cries waking the others, do we?'

Holm, in the next room, never slept, pacing the floor, hour after hour. The fellow on the other side cried all night long. The chloral was not always effective. Who, in this place, would be bothered by his whimpering?

Still, he was glad to find it was only a dream. Not like the other times.

That day in the railway carriage, for instance, when the man-bird flew in and perched on the luggage-rack above him, to warn of his impending death; or the time when the Pig stole his woman from him, laughing all the while. And he still shivered at the memory of the pink elephants climbing his bedroom wall, when the cocktail of drink and drugs drowned his sanity. Those visions were real enough, to him. He could not be called from them by the shake of an arm, and the sweet smile of his nurse, bathed in the morning light.

'And what were you dreaming of, Herr Munch?'

'A tiger and a bear were chasing me.'

'Ah, you see, a visit to the Zoo was not the most soothing experience, after all.'

'No, it was fine, truly. I assure you, I am all the better for it, just as the doctor said.'

It was true – the outing had been beneficial, as Jacobsen had predicted. 'An excursion on a fine day, to a pleasant destination – that is the next stage of your recovery. The Zoo is the perfect solution!' And the day had been fine, and the destination was indeed pleasant, after a gentle stroll down the lime-lined avenue, arm in arm with one of the Angels. Of course, he was not well enough to go alone yet, and it was reassuring to feel the support of her hand. Still, his limbs seemed to work properly, the paralysis a distant memory, and his lungs expanded at the taste of the fresh, scented air.

A photographer stood near the entrance, waiting to provide portraits, for a 'modest fee'. Munch imagined one of those half-page features the Gazette favoured. 'Edvard Munch, the famous painter, visits the Zoo.' The accompanying illustration would show him, spruce and healthy, beside an attractive young woman. They would think the painter was up to his old tricks again, not knowing his companion for a nurse. He had been lucky enough to be taken by his favourite Angel, the prettiest. Lise. A perfect adornment on a perfect day.

He had walked about, content in his physical improvement, glad to see innocence, where, before, all had been against him. The peanut seller did not yell at him. The man in the bowler hat hadn't followed him, though surely he could be a detective. The boy carrying balloons was interested only in the animals. The photographer did not conceal a revolver beneath his black cloth.

They moved amongst the exhibits, looking at the caged creatures, who looked back at them. He knew, now, what it was like to look out through bars. They chatted about what they saw.

'Which is your favourite, Lise?'

'Oh, the sea lions. They are so funny! And yours?'

'The tiger, I think. It has such power. And yet it does not look happy. Perhaps it is wrong to cage it... Perhaps it is wrong to cage any of them.'

'But it is a zoo, Herr Munch! That is what it is for!'

He laughed. He found himself laughing several times during the visit, something he had not done for a long while. The laugh, and the thought, filled him with wonder. Yes, it was indeed an uplifting outing.

Strange, then, that he should have had that nightmare. But, of course, in truth, the Zoo's inhabitants were incidental, except for the pig. The Pig was Heiberg, his rival; Heiberg was always the Pig. It was the woman who mattered, the woman who watched over their killing of him. Tulla, his old lover; Tulla, who had betrayed him, with Heiberg. It was always Tulla.

And, as if to prove he had not been harmed by them, he began to paint the animals that very day. It was a subject he had neglected in the past, but found surprisingly enjoyable. The doctor was pleased – 'Didn't I tell you my methods were the right ones, Munch? Plenty of sleep; good food; baths; and now, agreeable diversions.' Yes, despite the dream, the Zoo was a success. He would go again.

On his next visit, he was granted more freedoms. He was allowed to enter the Reptile House alone. Here, all colour was gone, and sound. He watched a small, black snake wind itself around a slender trunk, and run its forked tongue over its prey. Then, gradually, he began to hear a whispering all around him. Was it the Voices returned? Had he been wrong to think he was better? Then he realised it was the hissing of the snakes, coming out of their hiding places, entering his mind as he got used to the silence. Relief flooded through him. He had been foolish. Still, he left the House as quickly as he could, and rejoined his companion.

He asked her to climb to the top of the wooden observation tower, 'the highest in the world', according to the tourist brochure. Of course, he was not allowed to go himself, though suicide had never been his intention. He looked up at her, an Angel perched on high. When she came back down, he asked what she had seen. 'I have seen the world. I have seen how small man is! It is as if I have seen Creation!'

The boy with the balloons was there again. A child who lived close by, perhaps. This time, he sat with a sketchpad on his knees, before the pool. Munch leaned over his shoulder to see what he had drawn. The boy wrapped his arm tightly around his work. It was a response Munch could sympathise with. It was always difficult to take criticism. 'Herr Munch is a famous artist,' the nurse whispered to the Nanny. The boy paid no attention, biting his lip in concentration. 'Do you know that when the Zoo first opened they kept a sea lion in a bath tub?' Munch told him, reading again from his brochure. The boy smiled at this, but still would not look up. Munch let him be. He knew how deep the absorption into one's art could be He knew how necessary it could become.

And now Munch returned to his own work. He told Jacobsen he was planning a series of drawings based on his visits to the Zoo. The doctor was even more delighted with this further justification of his methods. To have restored emotional well-being to the holder of the 'Order of St. Olaf, first class' would surely enhance his reputation for curing artists. 'It will be accompanied by some text. I will use crayon – nothing too adventurous. A simple work, of a simple tale.' He knew what Jacobsen imagined. Fluffy animals, playing together – a picture-postcard vision.

He converted his room into a studio, placing his easels facing the wall. Like the boy, he preferred to keep his work hidden. Of course, the nurses looked from time to time. What they saw puzzled and disappointed them. He overheard their conversations… 'How can he be so famous, when his drawings are so basic? My little godson could do better! I cannot tell which animal is which. The tiger is recognisable, because of its stripes, but the others could be anything. Where is the bear? He said there would be a bear… All the animals were in front of him, in the Zoo. What does he mean by it all?'

Through the ferns, he watches the snake coil itself around the woman. They stare into each other's eyes, then kiss. He snatches the snake away and kills it with his bare hands, but soon she is kissing all the other animals on the island. The tiger and the bear tear each other apart in her presence. Still, she makes love to all the creatures she can find, and her children appear everywhere. Then the woman rides away on the back of a deer, leaving him alone, crying. When she returns, he kills her, and, as he does so, she looks up at him, and smiles. The animals gather around him. Large, small, fierce, timid – they are all there. Deer, monkey, sea lion. The pig is first, the pig with Heiberg's face. They crowd in upon him, and begin to tear at his flesh, with tooth and claw, pulling it from his bones, blood dripping from them. He screams, his face no more than a skull now. A screaming skull...

'Wake up, Herr Munch. I have been talking to you for the past five minutes and you haven't heard a word, lost in the contemplation of your drawings!'

He had been standing, looking over his finished work. He felt he had done well. He was enjoying the glow of satisfaction. A shame to be interrupted by a voice behind him.

Jacobsen. Jacobsen looking at the sketch in front of him. Of course, he understood more than the nurses. 'Burn it!' Munch heard his father's voice coming back to him through the years, demanding that he destroy his nudes. 'Are you mad, Edvard?' The fear of insanity, the curse of the family… echoed now by Jacobsen.

'Perhaps you are insane, after all. All the signs are here, in front of me – the absurdity of it all, depravity, obscenity. The humans are worse than the animals. Perhaps I was wrong in my diagnosis – in my cure. Burn them all!'

Of course, he will not listen. This time, he knows better. He is better. Jacobsen has healed his body, but art has healed his soul. Throughout its composition, he had been filled with a calm, such as he had never experienced before. And all he has done is tell a simple tale, a tale told many times before. The tale of the Creation, the Fall. Adam and Eve. His Alpha, his Omega. Tulla. The woman is always Tulla.

Finally, he is able to go out on his own. He has tried before, but was driven back by fear. The air pressed around him. The breeze became a whisper. But now he is fully well; soon he will go home. He goes to the Zoo – a last visit before his departure. It is as it was that first time; another beautiful day. Everybody is out enjoying the Spring sunshine, the early blooms, the playfulness of the animals.

The balloon boy is there again. This time, his sketchpad is on an easel, making it harder to conceal. Munch moves forward to look. The work is good for a child of that age. Carefully drawn; well executed. And the colours are straight from the discs on his palette. Bright blue, red, green. A solid background.

But the tiger is just a tiger.

The bear is just a bear.

The Zoo is just a zoo.

The Woman Who Never Begs

In the painting, the model sits there, lounging. The artist calls his work 'Reposing', but Magda doesn't like that. 'Lounging' is better.

She liked to lounge, in much the same place – a cushioned chair, in the bay of the window. A rocking-chair.

'Notice,' Paul said, gesturing at the picture, 'the light on the brow. As if she is alive.'

'I am alive,' Magda replied.

Did she know, then, that she would kill any rival brought to usurp her?

But she hasn't. All she has done is cut off two supplicant hands.

And she has suffered weeks, months, of painful forbearance – waiting until this morning's dawn, lying in cold, vengeful sheets – a second night when Paul had not come home. By then she had had enough, so she fetched a saw from the box under the sink, and begun her task.

It was harder than she expected. Back and forth with yellow, misshapen teeth; scrape, stick, drag. And there was blood. This surprised her. Straw, horse-hair; wax, paper; feathers stippling the air, sawdust drizzling to the floor. She had foreseen all these, but not blood. Perhaps she had imagined it, just as she imagined a cry. No-one came running, after all. All the neighbours remained silent – those who leer at her each morning after a night of pleading bed-springs, who lower their eyes after a convulsion of shouts and blows. So, yes, she must have imagined it.

Now, here she sits, cradling her prize, wondering why she had chosen to sever the struggling wrists instead of the single, unbending neck that was offered to her willingly, tauntingly. Surely a head was better? Weren't heads meant to be picked up in triumph, to be displayed for all to see? Wouldn't it have been perfect, to walk through the streets, carrying it by the hair?

'This is what I have done! This is what he has driven me to!' A Kokoschka moment – Paul had taught her so much about Kokoschka, his favourite artist. Kokoschka and his Alma, Alma as Gioconda, Alma in her red night-gown, Kokoschka and Alma together. Then 'Alma' lying on the floor, decapitated, drenched in red. Should she have done the same?

But no. That was all too histrionic. This is better.

After all, it was her own hands that beckoned him the night they met, catching his eye as she reached his drink across the bar.

'They are so beautiful. I would love to paint them.'

No more than an artist's chat-up line – she should be used to them, working in the Quarter – but she had fallen for it. Unlike all the others, what he said sounded real, so she followed him gaily home.

And almost at once, he wanted more. Canvas after canvas of face, bust, body; front, back, side; lying, sitting, standing, gathering dust in the corner. Naked – from discreetly coy to brazen full-frontal. Clothed – in dresses he bought for her, to magic her into whatever female incarnation he required.

The red party dress. The sanctimonious blue. The bridal veil.

Courtesan. Madonna. Bride.

Day after day of dressing, styling, posing.

Night after night of undressing, unravelling, abandonment.

But there was love, too. And domestic accord; she cooked, she cleaned! And respect, the first she had ever known. Why else would he teach her, talking to her, as he painted, of the places he had been to, the books he had read, and of art and artists, most of all. He took her to galleries, to illustrate their work. That was when he had shown her 'Reposing' – a painting she hated at once, without knowing why. But 'liking' did not matter, he told her. 'Appreciation is what counts. Understanding.'

And he would go on and on about the merits of a piece, so that, soon, she understood it was something artists enjoyed – educating, moulding, the girls they picked up from the street.

'The Pre-Raphaelites, Picasso! Kokoschka!'

And yet, who was he? How could he link his name with theirs? In all their time together, he had sold two paintings, and held one exhibition in the local hall.

Was that why, one day, he had brought this other home, and sat 'her' in the chair by the window? Magda's chair. Magda's place.

'It is to help you.'

'I have seen you are tired.'

'I have noticed you shivering.'

Yes, she was tired. The moments of lounging in the rocker had grown fewer. Yes, she was often cold, naked by a fire kept alight with no more than unpaid bills.

And there he was again, quoting those artists. 'Degas, Dali, Leonardo – they all use them.'

'Look,' and he rummaged through his art books, showing her first one, then another.

'Here… Millais's children in their bed. See, their faces are genuine. But, imagine, how could such little ones keep still for any length of time? So he replaced them with a mannequin. Who could tell the difference?'

She studied the picture. It was true she would never have known. Yet he had told her these artists sought nature and realism.

'It is a cheat. They are lying.'

'All artists lie,' he replied.

Still, at first, she welcomed this new presence. It was easier, that much was true, with a few hours of modelling-time freed. Freed by 'Sula'. Because, yes, Paul gave the 'woman' a name. Something else they all did, apparently. 'An affectation! Or just short-hand.'

Then, one day, stepping silently in from the market, she heard his voice. 'A visitor,' she thought, though there had been none before.

And there was none now. He was standing in front of Ullie, mouthing fervently, gesturing plaintively.

But was that so strange?

Hadn't she herself done it, moving about the house, making tea, or cooking dinner? A remark here, a question there. 'Colder today.' 'Now, where is the sugar?' (As if she would know, who had just arrived!)

Except it was no more than thoughts voiced into the steeping air directed instead towards the figure in the bay. Like talking to a cat or a dog.

What Paul was doing was different, she knew. It was… intimacy.

She began to watch them closely. It was easy enough. Her own chair had changed into the ladder-back in the darkest corner, its fraying wicker grating against her thighs. She saw the looks that passed between them. She heard their conversations, because, now, Sula answered in return. And every now and then, his foot would deftly strike the nearest rocker, so that the doll moved. Back and fore, it swayed, the daylight or street lamp fracturing the eyes, their shadows puckering the lips, so that it looked alive. So that it became a woman who could smile at him. Offer a kiss, perhaps.

Magda threw accusations at him, along with plates and cold cabbage stew. More raised voices for the neighbours to lower their eyes at.

'You look at her more than me, you look at her with desire!'

He said she was crazy. 'It is intensity. It is what I have to do. Look and look again until the creative spark is ignited.'

'You never look at me like that any more.'

'Have you seen yourself lately?'

Was that it? Was that what this was all about? That

she was no longer the perfect model? Unwrapping the mannequin, he had used the words 'pristine', 'unblemished'. She had thought they applied to its shop-bought newness. He had spoken such words to her, too, at her first sitting, their early bedding. But had not said them for a while.

After he had gone, she dragged the cheval to the bay, then fetched that first portrait – still there, of course; unsold. Her gaze shifted back and fore between the image and the mirror.

In the face of her reflection, fine lines were pencilled in by weariness and hardship. Two thick charcoal strokes gouged down from the lips, come overnight the first time he failed to return. The pouches beneath her eyes were smudged in purple. 'Crying is not good for the face,' Paul liked to say, before making her cry again.

And her body… The sweeping curves of the canvas were nowhere to be seen, lost in hunger and despair. Her skin was shaded with the patina of age.

And what of those 'beautiful' hands? Pitted and foxed as much as the glass in front of her, the chipped nails full of grime, the knuckles gnarling from the flesh.

From the rocker, Sula smirked like a dabbler's Mona Lisa.

Little by little, Magda faded from the paintings, legs, torso, arms.

Little by little, the mannequin took her place. Until only the eyes were real.

And, one day, pausing silently at the door again, she saw Sula sitting there, clothed in the red dress, nails painted to match. And Paul stepped from the shadows, and knelt down, as if in worship, and ruched stockings of the finest silk, inch by inch up each leg, caressing them, as he reached ever closer to their end. Once, he had wanted the same with her, but she had said no. Undressing, she could understand, but to dress again...? But Sula did not refuse… refused him nothing. She closed the door upon them.

The dress is beside her now, folded neatly. She removed it before fetching the saw, so there is no blood on it (well, of course, there is no blood!). She wants to keep it; it is hers. But the silk stockings she has burned. She watched them blacken and shrivel on a fire made from his brushes and palette – warmth, at last! There were other things she had done, too. Smashed his easel, cut up his clothes, thrown paint over the floor. China eyes followed her around the room as she worked, watched as she made a paste of red wine and flour to tip on the bed. From time to time a word was offered. 'Childish!' for the stamping and laughter. 'Clichéd!' – that was for the shredded suit.

And all the time Magda felt nothing.

'Catharsis – it can be a reason for painting, and for many other things, too,' Paul had told her, once. Another one of his educational lectures. 'Car-thar-sis.' But it was a word she couldn't understand.

And she still didn't understand when she took his canvasses from the corner and slashed each one from end to end.

It was waiting for Sula to speak of her failings. 'Fidgety, talkative, bored – what good is that in a model? I am far more reliable. I am the perfect muse.'

Waiting for 'He grew tired of you long ago. Your jealousy, your possessiveness.'

Waiting, finally, for 'Do you think I am the only one? Do you not know about the others he brought here when you were at the market, or in the bar? Real flesh and blood women that he tossed on that bed. The things he did with them that he never did with you… like the things he did with me that he never did with you…'

It was waiting for her to cut off Sula's hands.

Ahhh!

She examines one, then the other. Beyond the frayed

edges they are still perfect, the red nail varnish he had applied still intact, their surface smooth. The same cannot be said for the naked, handless doll that sits facing her. She is pleased about this. Pleased to see that Sula is not so perfect any more.

'Keep the harsh sunlight away!' Paul had commanded. But she would wait till he went out to pull the curtains wide.

'Idiot! Fool!' he screamed, the day she had dropped the poker on Ullie's protruding right ankle.

'It was an accident,' she replied. What else could it be?

The paint speckling was his – he was never a tidy artist. They would serve as age spots, scars.

So… no longer perfect at all.

Still, he could return it to the manufacturer, have it repaired, touched up. And he could buy more hands. There were shops that sold them.

Perhaps she should destroy it completely after all. Put it on the fire, perhaps. A real blaze!

No, the hands are enough. But there is something that must be done, first. She fetches more tools from the box, and drags the rasp over the skin. With the hammer and small chisel, she chips at the nails, until the varnish is scored, and the ends are hewn to the quick. There!

Then she places them together in the centre of the floor, as if in prayer. The red dress gets squashed into a bag, along with a few other belongings. Where will she take herself? The bar, perhaps? The neighbour with the dribbling leer? She doesn't know.

Magda closes the door, without looking back.

Behind her, Sula rocks in her chair. And smiles.

… In the painting, the model sits there… no, not lounging. She cannot lounge on the upright ladder-back chair. The street lamp flickers through the window, leaving its usual circle of light. Otherwise, she is naked. The debris of the room laps about her feet…

The work hangs in the city's most prestigious gallery, and has been sold for an 'undisclosed' sum. It is to be the first of a series, and its painter is famous, now, throughout the land.

The girl in the red dress looks at it, this way and that. Where she ends, and the other begins, it is impossible to see. He has put them together, skin and varnish seeped inseparably; flesh and plaster set fast forever; glue and blood coagulating within. Only the hands – or lack of them – mark themselves as Sula. They give the piece its name. 'The woman who never begs.'

If only she had killed her.

The Cabinet of Immortal Wonders

Jean-Baptiste Bécoeur is dancing with the flamingo again. A waltz – the dance has slunk across the border into Metz, even as far as the King's private chambers, it is whispered. 'Look,' he says, to his captivated audience, 'how beautiful she is! So perfect in her pink finery! So exuberant!' And then, as he swoops and twirls in his passion, a single feather floats to the floor. Jean-Baptiste stops.

The eyes of the peacock flick across to the tortoise, who moues in return. The macaque gibbers to the sloth, behind its long, elegant fingers.

A single tear slides down Bécoeur's face, meandering between a red pustule and a weeping sore. The birds in the Cabinet behind him bow their heads in sorrow.

'Jean-Baptiste! Jean-Baptiste!' His mother is calling him again. 'The Doctor is here.'

Which one is it this time? Dr. Jameau? Dr. Bertrand? Or an entirely new member of their tribe, come to try where the others have failed. Yes, a new one, because there is maman again, saying 'Jean studies birds!', the excuse she has proffered all the others, in explanation of his eccentric ways – the silence, his wanderings, his fascination with the morbid… the reasons for their visits.

What, first, did they think she meant? That he copied watercolours from his 'Histoire Naturelle', watched the sky through his spyglass from the attic window, gazed at the habitual lark in its gilded cage? 'All harmless enough' they would imagine, until he led them through to the nursery, that had become his study, and waved his arm towards his handiwork there.

He had seen their slippery words and fawning manners drop from them, then, as they stared at the crow slit from beak to tail, its entrails in a dish at its side; at his jars of dermistid beetles, moths and mice, waiting for his latest preparations to put an end to their lives; at the rotting turtle-dove on its perch, its eyes already gone, its feathers lying like a burst pillow beneath it.

How it made him smile to see their various attempts to avoid the stench, a hand or kerchief to the nose, in a pretence of sneezing, or a backward step towards the window or door!

'My apologies,' he would say, 'but it will improve. So far, I have been able to use nothing but what is available to hand… spices from the kitchen – cinnamon, pepper; tansy from the garden; turpentine, alcohol, camphor. Sadly, as you can see, none is sufficiently effective. But one day, when I am older, if I persevere with my studies, I will find a recipe for a preservative that will make my birds immortal!'

'Tut, tut, Jean, such talk is blasphemous! Why not, instead, tell monsieur le docteur how you capture your birds?' his mother would simper, encouragingly.

'There are various ways, monsieur. A noose for birds who walk on the ground. All one has to do is frequent a favourite feeding or nesting site. The birds are particularly vulnerable at their nest; it is quite easy to catch them then. For those who roost higher, birdlime is useful – spread on a branch, their claws become stuck fast to it, and they linger there until I can retrieve them. Unfortunately, my mother sometimes forbids my excursions, and then, by the time I reach them, they are already beyond my needs. Fresh is best, you see, monsieur. Alive to start, best of all.'

'Jean? Jean?' She has entered his room, now, and is shaking his arm. Why can't she let him get on with his work? Why can't she let him be? It has always been the same. These constant interruptions, accompanied by her eternal twittering. He has seen the mother birds behave in just the same way. Oh, the fuss as he approaches their chicks, as if by noise alone they could deflect him from his purpose! It is a cacophony almost as deafening as the trilling and chirruping of the lark in his nursery cage.

'Do you remember that first lark, maman? You put it facing my bed, thinking its song would sooth me! 'Ssht, Jean, ssht,' you would say. 'Look at the bird, how she sits there contentedly, and sings for you!' How I hated its perpetually open beak, its unfailing merriment! Do you remember when it died? How you thought the cat had strolled in and frightened it? But no, it was not the cat at all.

It was, simply, on that particular day, I could stand it no longer, so I opened the cage and removed the bird. With my hand wrapped round its throat, the beak moved in pitiful mime, but its heart pounded with a beat almost as loud as its song. A twist of its neck seemed to calm it, then another, and, finally, there was no sound at all. Peace at last! And I returned it to the cage, to stand it upright on its perch again, but it wouldn't stay! No matter how hard I tried, bending its claws, pummelling its body, it kept collapsing to the floor. And, already, its eyes were dull, and its feathers limp, their lustre gone. I could not understand it. I wanted to make it right. I wanted its beauty to return, for it to live again in its death, if that's what this was. Alas, I did not succeed then, but I have done so since! And soon, my achievements will be the envy of all who witness them!'

'Jean, it is I, Madeleine.' And so it is. The face in front of him shifts and shimmers, before steadying into a fixed shape. Not his mother, after all. Of course not – his mother has been dead these fifteen years. Buried in a box in the ground, for he was not allowed to preserve her in his Cabinet.

So, instead, here is Madeleine, his wife; but the doctor is real enough, though not Jameau or Bertrand, or that 'new' one – they too have long departed. Still, whoever this one is, like the others, he wants to see his 'patient's' creation, having heard, no doubt, of its wonder. For the Cabinet of Jean-Baptiste Bécoeur has improved a thousand-fold since those early days, with their childish attempts… a million times, even! He has learnt so much since then, his training as an apothecary put to good use, the years of experimenting with fifty different chemicals finally reaping their reward in his discovery of the perfect solution, the secret of eternal preservation.

'See,' he says to this latest man, 'how the birds perch effortlessly – so unlike that first lark! Others appear as if in flight. I use frames and wires to mount them, cunningly hidden by branches and shrubs. A stage designer from Italy has painted the background, so it is as realistic as possible. That is why I have added a few quadrupeds, to add to the sense of setting. The sloth, the monkeys, the deer. And insects – the 'food' for the other specimens. But it is the condition of the creatures that is the real success, the birds, especially. See how they remain unblemished after all these years, their coats pristine and shining! Of course, I outgrew the garden varieties long ago, and turned to the exotic. So picturesque, so fitting! The flamingo was brought to Metz from the south, by an itinerant dealer. The penguin has travelled even further! And look at the bird-of-paradise. My methods are perfect for such rainbow plumage, not simply preserving it, but enhancing it, even. Burnished gold, emerald green, ruby red – brighter than the hues nature gave it. Consider, also, the brilliance of the cardinal bird! It came from Surinam, and was destined for the Jardin des Plantes, but I was able to bid a higher price. The King would be jealous, I think, if he knew!

Ah, the King… Do you remember when the old king, his grandfather, came to Metz, Madeleine? August, it was… '44, I think – yes, he was on his way to the front, to see the War for himself. The entire town was so excited by his visit, then distraught at his sudden affliction, fearful of blame! And Louis was near death – prayers were given, there was talk of last rites. But I helped cure him, using my pharmaceutical knowledge. And though his standing was diminished afterwards, my name became famous throughout the land. It will be famous again, throughout the world, even, when my Cabinet is known! It is so much more than stuffed creatures displayed in a box! See how they live, how I have made them immortal. I am the only one to have done this. And through them, I will become immortal, too!'

'Jean, this is sacrilege! Only God has such power. The Bible says 'moth and dust doth corrupt' on earth. Man is not supposed to lay up its treasures, let alone…'

There, his mother is back again, quoting the gospels to him, as usual. Others have said much the same, some going much further, calling him an enchanter, a necromancer. The peasants, even, have whispered 'devil'… Ignorant yokels! Idiots! Jealous all, because he and he alone has vanquished the corruption of the flesh.

This man, this doctor she has brought, seems, at least, to appreciate what he has done, praising and wondering at each new discovery. 'The heron, the bustard! The humming-bird … amazing how it hovers, its beak within the flower, yet I see no means of suspension at all!' He flits about the Cabinet, examining everything, and ohhs and ahhs and coos in amazement – as enthusiastic as that first lark.

Too much so, perhaps? What if he is not really a doctor? How has Madeleine found him? Perhaps he is a rival come here to spy, to find out the secret of his recipe, so that he can steal it away, and become the most famous conservateur in the land. Come from the Museum in Paris, or across the border from Mannheim, for the Germans covet his work, too. Employed by the 'Academie'? Perhaps, even, Madeleine is in league with him, has had an assignation with him, and now they will run off together, taking his masterpiece with them.

And, sure enough, the man is no longer the strange doctor, but Levaillant, his former pupil, whom he once trusted, the one person he has shared his recipe with. 'Arsenic, Val! That is the key! So many trials and errors, until, finally… Other substances, yes – I mix it with camphor and potassium carbonate to form a soap… 'savon arsenical'! But white arsenic is the crucial ingredient. Eight ounces of it, for each finished portion. Strange that some call it a poison, strange that some say it debilitates and kills… But that is nonsense, nonsense! Otherwise, how would it preserve the birds, and make them look so well?'

Fool! He should have realised! Levaillant and Madeleine have become lovers. Together, they are planning to take the recipe and the Cabinet to the king! To reap the rewards that should have been his long ago. And before they go, they will kill him, and leave him here to rot…

…perhaps they have already gone, because rotting is what is happening to him.

Something shifts in his lower jaw. He puts his finger in his mouth, and feels the tooth give beneath it. Blood. Then, with a little push, the tooth has dislodged itself entirely. And another. And, examining the blood on his fingers, he sees that the nails are yellowed and striated. And his head… his head hurts so much!

But at least the Cabinet is still here – too large, of course, for easy removal – and the animals are all in place, and remain so perfect. Except for that one flamingo feather…

Jean-Baptiste roots about amongst the stones and creepers and shrubs, blinking closely, this way, that way, all around him. Ah, the eye of the lizard has fallen onto its rock, but it is made of glass, an artificial construct, not of the creature. And here, at the edge of a woven nest, another feather! Snow-white, this time, from the swan, surely – but it is only a down feather, like the flamingo's, and really, no more than would loosen through their everyday behaviour. A little squabble perhaps, an over-enthusiastic courtship dance. Now he finds the tooth of the badger, but that, too, is false – unlike his own, it is made of porcelain. No, on the whole, everything is in good order, everything is just as it should be. It is only he who spoils the show. For here is another tooth, dribbling from his mouth, tumbling down his waistcoat, on to the head of the disgusted peacock. And here, what is this hair? Long filaments of grey drape themselves over the leaves of the jacaranda. And there, the surface of the turtle-shell is dusted with flakes of desiccated skin. All fallen from his body, all witness to his decay.

He sees himself then, reflected in the mirror that serves as the drinking-hole he has provided for the animals. He sees a man far older than his years, his hair mostly gone, his cheeks sunk by the lost teeth, his skin covered in sores. He sees and doesn't see, for his vision comes and goes now. Just like his mind. Bécoeur sinks to the ground, and weeps silently – his body racked by dry sobs, because the arsenic has dried his tears. 'What have I done?' he asks the lizard. 'What have I done?' he screams at those who watch him from without, whilst banging his forehead against the glass.

'Come away,' Madeleine tells him, sweet, gentle Maddie, who has been faithful to him all these years.

'Help me, my love, help me, please!'

'Take my arm,' says Levaillant, the only one who has ever believed in him.

'You must rest,' says the kindly doctor, for, it seems, there is a doctor here, as well as his old assistant. 'And stay away from the poison. And from your specimens. It lingers on them still.'

But how can he stay away from his Cabinet, his own perfect world, his paradise?

Besides, it is too late now. The doctor knows it, in truth; and Levaillant – that is why he has returned, to be with him at the end. Madeleine knows it. That is why she is crying…

The flamingo and the toucan, the purple gallinule and the gentle dove – all have known for a long time. Only he did not.

Bécoeur is dancing with the flamingo again. No, no, no. It is Madeleine he dances with now. And there is no waltz.

Not even a minuet. A vague shuffle is all he can manage.

'This is foolish, Jean!' his pink feathered wife tells him. 'The doctor said you must stay quiet!'

'But it is good to dance, my little bird! Do you not know that dancing is an antidote to the poison? And music! Sing, my sweet! La-la, la-la-la!'

Yes, surely he has read this somewhere, in some journal, or paper. But, no, no, he suddenly remembers – that is what you must do if a tarantula has bitten you. And yes, he has one in his Cabinet, spinning its web between the bushes, and catching the flies and the moths, but it has never caught him. He has always been careful to avoid its den, just as he never steps near the scorpion, or the snake, that waits behind the mossy boulder, with its fangs visible, ready to pounce. None of these things has poisoned him. He has done that himself.

Still, his creatures are grateful for his efforts, for here they are, lining up on either side of the two dancers, applauding as they stagger past. The birds on one side, led by the royal swan, the quadrupeds on the other, led by the grinning monkey. To the left, the wings beat together, as furious as the humming-bird's; to the right, the paws clap together, in frantic union. And now, they are cheering, squawking, barking, howling, screeching, until their master collapses to the ground and his heart falters and stops, just like the lark.

Jesus in a Tree

Jesus is in the tree again. The second time this week.

'Look!' I say to Thomas. 'See! His eyes; the long hair draping over one shoulder. His beard.'

Thomas stands in the kitchen, looking at the sycamore by the hedge. The sycamore where Jesus appeared the Saturday before last. He (Thomas, not Jesus) shuts one eye, and moves his head this way and that. Next, he'll be framing the tree with his fingers.

'Does Jesus *have* a beard?' he asks.

As if that's all that matters.

When we moved here from the city, everything was going to be different. New house. New place. New life. The 'House of Hope,' he called it. The 'Palace of Platitudes,' I thought. But still, I wanted him to be right. I made a new 'to do' list, three tight-scripted pages long. But 'see Jesus in a Tree' wasn't on it, let alone 'debate his facial hair status'.

I dig up the icons buried deep in my memory. The cover of my grandmother's prayer book – a shepherd complete with crook and clamouring me! me! lambs. The crucifixes in every church I've ever been to. The films I've seen on TV. Seventy/thirty, I'm guessing, in favour of the beard. But then I think 'what on earth am I doing?'

It's not as if I'm seeing an actual man in the tree, a man who may or may not be Jesus. All I'm saying is that there's a head-and-shoulders image at the bottom of the sycamore, where, once-upon-a-time, it was cut. And for the past ten days, I've been thinking it looks like Jesus… sometimes. It's the light! It's the angle! I know these things! And, most of all, it's the rain. You could say that about a lot of things round here – crop success, crop failure, flooding. And now whether Jesus appears or not.

Which is why, the next day, He's not there.

'So where is He?' Thomas asks.

'I told you. He's not there all the time. It depends…on… certain…'

'You know He's got to be there every day, before we get the Church and media in.'

'What…?'

'They'll want to hear about this, after all. We could make a fortune out of it. Remember that peanut-butter sandwich? It went viral!'

And I realise he's making fun of me, and I can't help my eyes filling up, and he stops laughing and says 'Lydee? Are things okay?'

And I say 'Don't!' And rush into the garden.

Surely Thomas knows I'm not the kind to have visions, in sycamores, peanut-butter sandwiches, or anywhere else. There's been no 'seeing the light' moment. I've never had those, not even in my 'religious' phase, which happened around fifteen, like most things. True, I got myself confirmed, but then it passed, along with all those other teenage fads, such as being in love with a pop-star; having a pash for an older girl in the school. Wanting to be a brain-surgeon, save the planet. 'Get married' wasn't on my list back then, either, until I met Thomas. And everything else got crossed off, until we walked down the aisle. Which was when I added 'HAVE A BABY!!!!' And not just one. Or two. But three, or four. Four, to make up for my own dysfunctional family. Why not? It was going to be wonderful! It was going to be so easy!

Suddenly it's the opposite of everything that's gone before. All that 'being careful' and, now, what are you? Care-*less*? Crazy – because suddenly you care more than anything in the world. You want; you need; you must. Still, at first, as the months go by, it's something you joke about, almost. Those things you talk about doing, then do.

Watching your cycle, checking your temperature, standing on your head. Then, as more time passes, there's the visit to the G.P. 'Try this, try that, try the other.' Then the hospital appointments start, with all their questions, their tests. This …oscopy; that smear; that scan. It's the biggest 'to do' list I've ever had! So many ticks!

But still a BIG BLACK 'X' at the end.

Still no baby.

'You've got to believe. Never give up hope. You've got to have faith!' Which of the men in white coats said that? After which failed attempt?

And I went from his clinic, holding Thomas's hand, singing 'you gotta have faith!', like some soul brothers' chorus line, or evangelist's mantra. And I've been singing it ever since, through every month that's passed, every failed cycle, and every fortune spent.

And I thought Thomas was, too.

And when we came here, I thought that's what it was about – that he hadn't given up. (That 'new *life'*!) This was his way of signing up again. All those books he'd been reading about getting back to nature, healthy living – weren't they to do with *It*? 'This is a place where things flourish, blossom, thrive.' Wasn't that what Thomas was thinking? That's why he planted all this fruit and veg (organic, of course!). How could anything survive in the city, with all that concrete, steel and glass? All that *pollution*!? But all around here, there's so much growth. Abundance. Luxuriance. So couldn't a baby grow, too? Like it couldn't grow before? There'd be more chance. And yes, of course, there was the money. We'd spent so much! But, coming here, we'd get a far better place, and have some extra cash for more treatment.

I thought.

But now I don't know; I'm not so sure. Lately, Thomas doesn't want to hear about percentage chances, new treatments. Alternatives. Perhaps that's not why Thomas came here at all. Now I wonder if he came here to draw a line. He says things like 'putting the past behind us'; 'moving on'. And now I'm guessing he means 'moving on without…'

So here I am, standing outside the back door, breathing in all this fresh air, surrounded by nature, seeing Jesus in a tree – except I'm not. Already, from here, it's not so clear. From the kitchen is best, after it's rained. Still, I think, since I'm out here, I may as well take a closer look. Sure enough, when I'm right by the sycamore, it's just a broken tree. The edge where the trunk was cut is folded like a poorly-healed scar. This cut bit forms the shape – from the shoulder, round up the hood, then down again. Beneath it, there's a gnarled bit, with whorls and indentations, as if it's been carved. And some of these are black. I don't know what the black is. Thomas is the one who's supposed to be the nature buff. Some kind of fungus, perhaps? It's the black that makes Jesus, intensified by the rain. But since it's dry now, there's little to see. And there's no beard. So that solves that problem. Solves every problem – I wish.

Then Jesus speaks to me. 'Hi, Lydee!' – which is strange on two counts. First, that He says 'Hi', and second, that He knows my name. The 'hi' thing – well, I guess it's possible that Jesus moves with the times, or something like that. That He's not Jesus as was, but has had a second coming, so uses contemporary jargon. But if that's true, wouldn't He also change his looks, so that they're up-to-date as well? Shouldn't He be in jeans and a hoodie? But, if that's the case, I wouldn't have decided the image looked like Jesus. This is getting complicated.

And then there's the name thing. 'Lydee', not even Lydia. Like He knows everything about me. But isn't He supposed to know everything about everybody? Or is that just God? Omni…whichever. Still, He's God's son, so perhaps they pass on personal information. Perhaps it makes sense that He knows my name. But 'hi' and just the fact that He's talking to me…well.

I've said all along that I'm not really seeing Jesus, but, suddenly, I'm hearing voices, really hearing voices. So now I'm wondering if Thomas is right to be worried after all. What if there is something wrong with me? Like before.

Then Dan-next-door pops out from behind the hedge. 'Hope I didn't startle you. What are you up to?'

'I was looking for Jesus.' I shouldn't say this. I know it as soon as the words come out of my mouth. It's one of the things I do – speak without thinking. Once upon a time, Thomas said it was one of the things he loved about me. He doesn't say it now. But this isn't Thomas, anyway. It's Dan. And Dan laughs.

'Does he live around here, then?'

I've never really noticed Dan before. It doesn't sound as if he's mocking me – just joking about it. He hasn't backed away, as if he's thinking 'Woah! There's something not right, here!'

So I think I should just come clean. I show him the sawn-off trunk. 'See – the hair, the eyes. Except…it's not so good close up. But from the kitchen window, in the rain, it looks like him…whatever He looks like…'

I know I'm babbling on, but Dan just laughs again, and says 'Yes, I see what you mean. There's a stone in my garden, which looks like Mahatma Gandhi. I'll show you sometime. Once I saw a bird shape in a cloud. I was the only one who could see it.'

As easy as that, Dan believes me. No doubts, no questions, no funny looks. Dan believes me, though he hardly knows me. Whereas Thomas is married to me, and has known me forever. How can that be?

Dan disappears back through the hedge, and I am left alone with Jesus. Or, rather, I'm left alone with a broken tree. I put my hand on the pitted bark. I am touching Jesus, you could say. What if, deep down, in a tiny part of me, I do really think this will fix things? That this will put whatever doesn't work properly inside me right again? I guess this is what Thomas is afraid of – that I'm getting religion, and next it will be mumbo-jumbo, witchcraft…a lucky rabbit's foot! Lucky pants! Perhaps he thinks I'm looking for a miracle. Perhaps I am, but it's nothing to do with God. Just us.

Still…

And I'm still there, when it's getting dark, holding on to the tree, till Thomas comes to look for me, and leads me back inside.

Yesterday, Thomas went into town and bought an axe. 'This is part of his back-to-nature idea. He doesn't want a chain-saw, with its noise, vibration, fumes. He wants to feel the connection between blade and tree – metal against wood. He wants to turn the cutting of a tree into a ritual.' This is what I might have thought just after we came here. Now I'm thinking: 'Why has he bought an axe? Why is he looking at the Jesus tree with one eye closed again?'

But why would I care if he cuts the tree down? Since I don't believe in Jesus anyway?

Yes, I care.

Because if he does, it will be over. There will be no chance of him saying 'Yes, of course, Lydee. I can see exactly what you mean. And everything you've ever said in our lives together is true. And one day, we are going to have a baby!'

Of course, you could say the tree itself doesn't really matter – it's just a symbol. And if it's cut down, there could be something else to take its place, after all. Something else that I see, say, or do – that I tell Thomas, and want him to believe in.

'It's going to be a beautiful day today' when black clouds are gathering above the hill.

'I'm going to make bread. I know I've never made

it before, and I'm a hopeless cook, but it's going to be wonderful, and we'll never have to buy shop-bought again!'

Something small.

Something big.

'I'm swimming the channel, Thomas.'

'I'm climbing Everest.'

'I'm going to the moon!'

'Yes, Lydee. You are. Of course you are. And then we're going to have a baby!'

'There's a pig flying over the barn, Thomas.'

'Yes, Lydee. And we're going to have a baby.'

But now Thomas is heading for the tree – even though it's raining – and I know he's never going to believe any of those things. And I remember now, from those long-ago confirmation classes, that Thomas was the disciple who doubted Jesus. And it looks to me from here as if Jesus is crying, though I know his tears are just droplets of rain. Is He crying because He knows what's going to happen? That Thomas is going to cut into his neck? That He is going to die – again?

Or is He crying for me?

Watching me Watching you

Somewhere in the deepest reaches of the planet, a creature without a face nuzzles in the ooze and the dark.

When I first read there was such a thing as a faceless animal, I imagined a body without fur, with four limbs, a tail and, I guess, a featureless head. And I pictured it in the depths of some jungle cavern, where no light or sound entered, and no more than an occasional sigh of air. It was almost a disappointment to discover it was a brainless daub of matter, not that far down in the ocean. Amphioxus, also known as the lancelet. A sub-phylum of Cephalochordata. Or… just a fish.

But then I began to picture what *it* might look like, along with all other similar species – and asked myself whether they counted, anyway, because they weren't vertebrates, like us. That's my problem, I suppose. I make too much of faces, whether they exist or not. Except, for me, they'll always be there.

I've started with the story of the fish, because I know you like animals. I know a lot about you, but now I want you to know about me. I could begin with the usual list of likes/dislikes/favourites you'll find on any dating/matching/soulmate website – colour, music, food and all that. But that's not what this is about. I want you to *understand*. Still, my favourite film might be useful here – it's that one with John Travolta and Nicholas Cage, where the bad guy gets a plastic surgeon to swap his face for the good guy's. It seemed far-fetched when it first came out; it happens, now, all the time. I should also tell you, if I'm honest, that I don't really like animals – or rather, I have no particular feelings about them. It's the faceless bit that matters in the fish story.

By now, you'll be getting the picture. I have a 'thing' about faces – well, I guess we all do, to an extent. Think of a baby's connection with its mother, or our fascination with the Mona Lisa. Or how, in the film, swapping just the face is enough to carry the deception, even with the good guy's wife. We fix on what's above the neck. With me, it's more than a fixation, it's a physiological disposition – or neurological, if you prefer, since it happens inside my brain, a particular part of my brain. It's called the Fusiform Face Area, or FFA for convenience, and it's located in the ventral stream of the temporal lobe. Or at least that's what the experts think; the science is surprisingly new. All I know is I've been like this since childhood. My mother used to call it my super-power. It's something mothers do to comfort a child, when they realise they're different. Unless she was shouting at me for talking to strangers. 'What's a stranger?' I asked, the first time it happened. 'Someone you don't know.' 'But I do know them,' I insisted. 'I see them all the time, wherever we go.' And I had.

Back then, we lived in a small town. Small, but bigger than the kind where you say 'everybody knows everyone else'. After a couple of years, we moved to a bigger place. It made no difference. Wherever we went, whatever the size of the population, it didn't take long before I knew them all.

Today, I'm sitting outside a café in York, looking for a guy called Michael. Michael has friends in the city. He used to enjoy visiting them, which is why his family think he might have come here now. Michael walked out of his home a month ago. His photo came up on a Missing Persons website, with mention of a large reward. I don't like doing this for the money, I'm not a private detective, but a man's got to live, and there's not much else until the divorce comes through.

All I have to do is sit here, having cappuccino after americano, with a croissant or bagel now and then, and stare at the crowd passing in front of me. It's what a lot of people on their own do, anyway – those who don't read newspapers or endlessly check their phones. People-watching, it's called. But all they'll see is a blur of faces, unless someone passing close has a distinguishing feature – a scar, tattoo, that kind of thing. Or unless they pick out an actual acquaintance, which isn't likely in a strange place.

With me, it's different. I can scan a crowd of a dozen, a hundred, a thousand faces, and match one to someone I've no more than glanced at before. Or seen in a photo, or on television. Or known, but not seen, since childhood. You know those celebrity 'before they were famous' type photos? They're as easy as a childhood game of 'Snap' to me. Put simply… I never forget a face.

So if Michael appears in the street today, I'll know it's him, even though I've seen no more than a grainy picture – that's all his family had, which, of course, embarrassed them greatly. So different from yours, who had photo after photo of your warm, smiling face 'because she's so special to us.' Which is why, perhaps, you became special to me. Which is why I'll be keeping an eye out for you, even though Michael's my main concern right now, because it's something I always do.

'Another coffee, sir?' The waiter's been flicking his dish-cloth on my table for a while, now. I guess he wants me to move on. I guess he feels I haven't spent enough money to justify sitting here for three hours. With so many people about, he's after a more profitable customer, someone who'll give him a big tip, best of all. And yes, I'm happy enough to relocate to the diner across the street and move indoors, since it's starting to rain. Rain doesn't affect my powers of recognition, you'll be glad to know. Most things don't. You could have changed your hairstyle, coloured it, started wearing glasses and I'd still know you anywhere… though a face-transplant, or a criminal's balaclava might pose something of a challenge. Super-powered, but not super-human.

So it doesn't matter that water is streaming down the windows of this new place, or that everyone outside is rain-smeared and they have their collars pulled up, or umbrellas low. I'll still recognise Michael (and you) if he appears. That's something I have over cameras. There are plenty of those around here – on that corner, outside the café I just left, attached to every other lamppost. But the lenses will be mottled with grey water by now, and the images they produce will be compromised. Yet even when they're as sharp as an up-to-the-minute HD television, I, and the others like me, have a better record of successful identification. It's nice to know humans are still able to out-perform new technology in some areas, whether it's CCTV or the newest facial recognition systems which are beginning to pop up everywhere. Did you know that FRSs have played a role in modern law enforcement far longer than we 'super-recognisers' (that's what they call us, by the way)? No, I don't suppose you did.

And I don't suppose you know how many missing people there are in this country, either, even though you're one of them. Over one hundred and thirty five thousand in England and Wales in 2015/16. Imagine that. All those people out there, just… gone. Left their homes, travelled elsewhere, on foot, by car, bus or train. Wandering about, some of them – quite a lot of them, in fact. Eighty per cent of adults who leave have some kind of mental health problem. Most of them don't go far. Others go with a fixed purpose of where they're heading, what they are going to do. Kids, mainly, aiming for the bright lights, away from the small towns and small-minded parents. Either way, they're all still gone… gone, but not forgotten. And that's the trouble. We all have to 'respect the right of adults to go missing', as the guidelines say. Michael, for instance, left of his own accord, no foul play suspected; it could be he doesn't want to be found. But it's hard for those left behind. They want him back, desperately, even though they'd only taken one fuzzy pic of him in years.

That's what got me into this. When I began in the Department, it was all to do with spotting criminals, having to be aware of the worst things men (and women) are capable of, while witnessing the suffering of their victims. Until, in the end, I couldn't stand it any more. So I moved to tracing missing people, because there was something so worthwhile in returning the lost to their loved ones. Or, if they don't want to go back, at least letting the family know they're okay. And it all went well enough until I saw a photo of you.

I've given up on Michael for today, now – the rain got so much worse, the crowds were thinning. Some might say it was a waste of time, but I did spot a persistent shop-lifter, and reported him to a heavy-lidded, slack-jawed, store-detective. I'll get a reward for that. I'd seen the thief's mug-shot on the news last week – another snatched, watery CCTV image, but enough for me. The detective didn't believe me at first, but at least it made him open his eyes and shut his mouth.

I spend a lot of time watching local news when I'm back in my B and B, or boarding-house room, which is where I am now. When I passed through reception, the owner said 'Are you enjoying our beautiful city, sir?' 'Yes,' I replied, it seemed the polite thing to do. I didn't like to say I hadn't seen the Minster, or visited the Viking Museum, or paid any attention to 'the great shopping experience that York has to offer'. None of these things holds any interest for me, I'm too busy focusing on the faces that float around them. Once upon a time, Marie and I visited Stonehenge. Afterwards, she asked me what I thought of it. 'Smaller than I expected,' I replied, because I knew it was something people say. I couldn't tell her I hadn't really noticed the monoliths – I'd been too busy tracking a persistent drug-dealer, who'd come up on our screens the week before. Besides, a stone is just a stone.

I may go back out later, round the pubs, for another trawl.

Or maybe not. But for now I'm just lying on the bed talking to you.

I know what I should be doing. I should be getting out Marie's letter again, reading it properly this time, along with the decree… whichever, citing her reasons for wanting a divorce. Another woman – it always is, isn't it… or most of the time. Someone younger, though not too young in this case, certainly no sixteen year old girl, and more attractive – beautiful, I would say. Someone from work – that's another favourite, isn't it? Someone I got involved with in work. Such a cliché. This is how Marie's telling it – to her friends, our families, and now, it would seem to the courts. And I don't blame her for that. In fact, I should be glad of it – it's simpler, it makes more sense. Clichés are easier to understand. And how to explain it otherwise?

The man with the broken nose, the girl with the red hair, the boy with the pouting lips, the woman with the narrow eyes, the woman with the wide eyes, the man with the receding hairline, the man with the hood pulled down over half his face. The old man, the young man, the middle-aged. The unhappy looking teenager, again and again and again. 'Look, look at them,' I said to Marie, when I was trying to explain. 'Image after image, row after row; scroll down and down and down, page after page after page.' This is what I was looking at day after day after day. And I would take them home with me, every evening, inside my head, my mind like a carousel of slides, each one with a face on, going round and round.

'Did you remember to stop for milk on the way? And bread, and coffee?' Marie would ask, when I got in. But no, I hadn't remembered. I could recognise the guy I'd been in primary school with, and hadn't seen in thirty years, until I came across him on platform nine in Paddington. He, of course, had no idea who I was. I can remember that the girl pulling pints in the 'Lion' was the same girl who waited table in the Harvester ten miles away two years before. 'Hello,' I said to her, 'How's it going? Better, now you're closer to home?' The look she gave me… I think she thought I was stalking her. But no, I can't remember three things Marie told me to get on the way from work. And no, I don't know what the heroine in the TV drama said to her boyfriend in the last scene. 'We're supposed to be watching this together!' Marie shouted. 'It's like you're never here, even when you're sitting beside me.' Of course, I'd been too busy thinking it was the same actress who was on a day-time magazine programme on children's TV back when I was a kid.

'It's not easy for me, either,' I tried. 'It's as if I can never rest. And it's not my fault – I was born like this.'

That glitch in a tiny part of my brain, which could have gone either way…

'Do you know that there are others just the opposite of me? But they get a Greek name to describe their condition, along with treatment and sympathy…'

Sometimes I wonder what it's like to be those others, to be face-blind. To meet someone, then forget them straight away. A kind of 'how-do-you-do?' Groundhog Day. Some of them don't even recognise their own family members from one day or the next. Imagine… except I can't. It's beyond me, just as, I guess, I'm beyond them. Still, there must be something peaceful about it, I can't help thinking. To have a mind empty of people, instead of all these clamouring images. To know no-one, instead of knowing every person you've ever seen.

The boy with the tooth-heavy smile. The girl with rat-tailed hair. Face, after face, after face, because, really, none of these distinguishing characteristics matters. They're all faces I will remember, even the most non-descript, distant, bland. All still going round and round and round.

Then one of those slides shot forward, into place, and lit up the screen, or perhaps some hidden, as yet undiscovered part of my fusiform gyrus. And the others didn't seem so important after that, and neither, I suppose, did Marie. She was simply too familiar. There was no thrill in catching sight of her across a crowded room, and there should have been, even after fifteen years of marriage. And so much of that time was spent looking at other women, though, in fairness, looking at men, too. 'Watcha looking at, mate?' – it's been said to me so often. Once, a guy punched me, because he thought I was coming on to him. And then there's the jumping off buses because I'd seen someone from the files. Or that day we were on a train to Brighton, and I got off at Gatwick Airport because I knew I'd recognised someone on the station platform. Just leaving Marie sitting there, while I chased after a ghost, leaving her alone. 'But I'm always alone,' she told me, when I finally got back to her.

So I can't really blame her for asking me to go, at the start of the year. And I couldn't really argue when the Force suggested I take some 'gardening leave' at around the same time. I wasn't concentrating, I was too distracted… or… I was too focussed on just one case. Wanting to know all the background information about the disappearance, the when/where/how, and questioning always the 'why?'; wanting to travel the country on the flimsiest of reasons, when before, all I needed was to match a photo and a face. So, yes, someone from work, just not a colleague, someone younger and more attractive than my wife. But someone I've never even met, never even seen, in person, though I've tried and tried and tried. You.

I think it was getting Marie's letter yesterday that got me started talking to you. After all, there's no-one else about. But neither are you, except for the giant, lit up picture in my head, together with all the other things I've learnt. It's not so unusual for a cop to get obsessed – you know, the kind who spend years trying to solve a single cold-case, or the undercover guys who lose sight of which life is really theirs. And it's not so strange for people in general to get hung up on one missing person. It's the way of the world, in fact. In the U.S., for instance, the greatest number of missing kids are black teenage boys, but nobody pays them much attention. But if a pretty, white girl (usually with blond hair) disappears, well, the whole nation gets involved, posters everywhere, praying, ribbons on trees, physically searching. We're not much different over here, when you think about it.

I'm not sure how common the talking bit is. I just felt it would make you more real, somehow. Not just a face, even though that's what you're supposed to be.

Such a nice face, though. I knew it the moment I saw it, that moment the slide shot out. And you were asking something of me, I was sure, asking me with your funny blue eyes, your warm mouth – those features I wasn't supposed to notice because that wasn't how my mind worked. You were asking me to do something no-one else had done – find you, and make it all right. There was so much that was different about you, even though everyone else said no, it wasn't so. 'There are hundreds, if not thousands, just the same.' You went of your own accord, no foul play suspected (like Michael) – you'd closed all your bank accounts the week before, and packed a travel-bag. You weren't in a relationship, there'd been no family quarrels. 'A perfect daughter,' said your parents. 'We're so close,' sniffed your sister. 'Got on with everyone,' all your colleagues agreed. 'The kind of person who stands out in the crowd,' your friends said. And yet… not a single sighting. Not one, in nine years. Just as if you'd disappeared off the face of the planet. 'Gone abroad,' Pete, my partner, said. 'Straight away, to start a new life.' But there was no record of departure, or sightings at airports or ports. And 'abroad' is something I can't deal with. I have to leave the world alone. This small country is big enough, when you're looking for one particular face. Out there, six hundred and seven people disappear every day – that's over four million in twenty years! We all have to give ourselves some boundaries, hard as it can be sometimes. 'She's dead, mate.' Another of Pete's helpful suggestions – something I can deal with even less. 'Gotta be, after nine years. Sorry, and all that.' But, no, you're not. I know it. You're out there, waiting for me. Somewhere.

So I packed a bag of my own, and started visiting this town, that town, at weekends, or in work-time, on the pretext of another case. Going anywhere that you had any slight connection with, any place mentioned by your family or friends. And that was something else I shouldn't have been doing – I got involved with your family on a personal basis, when, in fact, all I was supposed to be was a back-room boy. 'I'll find her,' I told your parents. 'I promise.' And I know I shouldn't have said that, and that, really, I was promising myself. That's how I learnt you like animals. Well, of course you do. Someone with a warm, loving nature always does. And they told me your favourite colour/food/film/book/music ('anything that may give me a clue would be useful') – all those things I don't need you to know about me. I'll be able to fill you in on all of them, when we finally get together. For now, it's just this business of getting you to see where I'm coming from. This thing that happened, because I saw your face.

I'd like to think that's not so strange, either, though perhaps in a different way from the norm. All those romances based on love at first sight. Or Helen launching a thousand ships. Okay, perhaps it's not so good to have a marriage break up over it, but at least you didn't start a war. Besides, it doesn't look as if Marie and I would have made it anyway.

So I don't want you to blame yourself for the split, even if Marie is – like I say, she does that because it's easier than explaining my condition. 'You're crazy!' she said the last evening I was there. I don't think that was fair. 'Me, and the other 1 to 2 per cent of the population?' I replied. That's how many of us there are supposed to be. The same percentage, strangely enough, of our counterparts, the sufferers of prosopagnosia. 'Stop blaming that tiny part of your brain,' she screamed. 'This doesn't happen to all the rest of them!'

Okay, perhaps I'm an extreme-recognizer, or something like that. Perhaps my cortical activation is overly sensitive. If that's possible. But it doesn't mean I'm crazy, does it? Searching for you from one end of the country to the other doesn't mean I'm mad. Or loving someone I've never met. Happens all the time these days, with internet dating, and the like. 'But that's a two-way thing, even when they're faking their identities! She doesn't even know you exist!' Another of Marie's parting lines.

But now I'm talking to you, that's all changed, hasn't it?

I think I'll say 'goodnight' now. It's been a long day, and my eyes are tired from screen-scrolling – I've been looking out for you on social-media, while we've been chatting. Nothing. But tomorrow's another day.

I dreamed about you last night. I do, all the time. It's so much better to have just the one face spooling through my night-time thoughts, especially as it's yours. A shame, perhaps, that it was more of a nightmare – the kind we all get now and then – chasing after something that keeps one step ahead, or disappears around the next bend, to vanish altogether, just as you reach out your hand. The 'something' was you, of course. And your face looked back at me, then waited right up close to me, lips reaching towards me, and then… pouf! you were gone. That's when I woke, heart racing, body sweating. But it's just a dream, isn't it? It's not going to come true. What's going to happen is quite the opposite. I'll see you, you'll see me, and everything will be all right. I just don't know when.

I phoned Marie after I showered. I think the dream unsettled me. Or perhaps I needed someone to talk back to me, to hear another voice.

She told me you'd been found. Not dead, no; very much

alive. A new life, in fact, born again nine years ago with the money you stole from the company you worked for – something they kept secret, 'for financial reasons', or plain embarrassment. I didn't hear much after that.

Words like bitch, and liar and thief, and fool, fools, FOOL, YOU STUPID FOOL! Changing tunes, taking for rides, pulling the wool… but the line was bad, and Marie's jealous, isn't she? And the press are always keen to see the worst in a person – it makes better copy, after all. And I guess your family are just in shock.

But they don't know you, like I do. I think they've all got it wrong.

It's even possible that someone swapped faces with the real you, like in the film. But I can't work out where that leaves me, since it's your face I love. And I don't know who I'm talking to any more.

The Woman who Turned out to be Me

I choose the café with the red geraniums. Three to a box; three boxes in a row. It's something I like to do – pick out some gaudy, catchy detail, so that I can snag it in my brain. To remember.

And yet… he's not here.

The café with the red geraniums, around the corner from the library, down the street from the station. I'm in the right place, aren't I? Yes, surely… but still, there's no-one around, except me. Oh, and another woman sitting just the other side of the glass, who must have come in while I was studying the menu. Taking my time, turning the single sheet over and back again, humming and hahing, because… he's not here.

'This is Russell Street?' I ask the waiter, who's tapping his pencil on his notepad, his toe on the ground. That means impatient because I'm taking so long.

Still, there could be another café with red geraniums in another street. It's not especially unusual. It's not such a strange question. Is it?

He – the waiter – rolls his eyes skywards. That's okay, stupid this means. It's one of the few expressions I understand, because I've known it all my life.

Stupid, because I didn't know any of my class-mates. A moron, because I'd forget where I lived, or say hello to people I'd never met. Stupid, because I didn't spot that my husband of twenty-five years was having an affair. No, that one doesn't count, because it really was stupid. It's nothing to do with that tiny part of my brain, in 'the temporal lobe of the fusiform gyrus, where facial recognition and, possibly, location awareness, takes place'… Or is it?

The waiter is waving his arm up towards the left. I'm okay with body gestures, which is why I knew what the pencil-

and-toe tapping signified, which is why I look up, following his hand. Ah, the sign is there. Russell Street. Good.

'Cappuccino,' I say, just to get him out of my hair, my perfectly-coiffed new hair-style, done just yesterday, that mustn't be mussed up. Why doesn't he go and bother the other woman, the only other customer? Woman, not a man – I know that much! Not the man I'm supposed to be meeting here.

Still, I'm in the right café, in the right street, apparently. Of course, I was here yesterday, straight after the hair appointment, and the day before, which is probably why the waiter thinks he's dealing with an idiot. He recognises me, but I don't recognise him. But then again… perhaps he's not the same guy.

And the time is right. I've checked and checked. But now it's getting wrong – with each minute that passes he's late, late, later… not coming. Three coffees on, and John's still not here.

'John… couldn't he have thought of something more original?' I take Jenn's voice with me wherever I go. It helps, I find.

I used to take Richard, back when we were married – Richard, in the flesh, which helped, even more. He was good at touching my elbow, whispering in my ear. Such a caring husband, I thought, until I discovered he was whispering into another woman's ear, at the same time.

Now, I have Jenn's voice. It's better than nothing, I guess.

'This way, mother. This is your house.'

'That's your neighbour, mum. Better say 'hello'.'

'It's me, mum. Jenn, your daughter. Remember?'

But I don't.

Not her face, anyway.

'You're too pretty,' I've told her. 'No distinguishing marks or features to help me out.'

‘What does that say about Dad, then?’ she asked me, once, when she was younger. Her father, with his nose broken from an old rugby injury, and his thick, bristling brows.

‘Perfect for me,’ I thought, the first time I saw him. Strange that he turned out to be perfect for someone else, too – though I’ve heard he’s plucking his eyebrows now, or she’s doing it for him.

‘John’ hasn’t got any conspicuous features, either. A foolishness, on my part, considering; vanity, rather, that a fifty-year old divorcee should want to meet someone handsome. Or is it simply that I don’t trust ‘characterful’ looking men any more?

‘For god’s sake, you can’t believe that photo, just like you can’t believe his name’s ‘John’. No-one puts their real selves on these sites.’

‘I did.’

‘Yeah, well… your photo and your name, maybe. You just omitted to mention the face-blind thing.’

And she’s right.

It was Jenn who insisted I meet ‘John’ in a public place, somewhere I’d visited a few times, to ‘get a handle on it’. Jenn has never really understood how my mind works – or doesn’t work. This is my third visit to Café Bernice, and it’s still as if I’ve never been here before, even with the geraniums.

I touch the petals of the plant nearest to me. Scarlet velvet, a tart’s dress. I don’t understand how the flowers look so good, flaunting themselves. Mine, back home, are streaked with black, on top of brown, rotting stalks. Dead-heading – I think that’s something I’m supposed to do, but never get round to. And feed, I guess. These ones probably get some kind of high-powered chemical product. Perhaps I should try it, or at least some organic variety. Seaweed – I’ve heard that’s good. I’ve heard…

‘Mum, he’s not coming. Give up, won’t you?’

She's right, of course. He wouldn't be an hour late; half an hour, maybe, but not an hour. I start pulling my things together. I put a five pound note down for the waiter, thinking he won't care how stupid I am, as long as he gets a good tip – and he'll welcome me next time I come. Looking up, I catch the eye of the woman opposite. She's doing the same thing, too – stuffing her purse into her handbag, getting ready to depart. That's when I realise she's me.

She walks past the sorry geraniums, cowering around her porch. Inside, she stands in front of the bathroom mirror, looking at the woman who must be her. It has to be, doesn't it? The face is no more than a wash-basin's width away. The square, shiny object she's looking into reflects the window behind – not just the person near it. She raises her finger to touch the smooth, flat surface, and another finger touches her own. It has to be a mirror. So, yes, it has to be her.

In the café, it was different. She didn't realise there was glass between the outside tables and the inside area. She thought it was a continuation of the same space, some out, some in. There was no reason for her to think the other woman could be her, until those last few minutes, when they began to move together, like a pair of land-locked synchronized swimmers.

Of course, it had happened before. A mirror in a store, shop-windows as she rushed down a street. She had said 'hello' to herself on several occasions, thinking there was something familiar about the other woman, so she should greet her to be on the safe side. Better to be overly sociable than rude, she had decided a long time ago. It can even happen with photos, when she's looked at holiday snaps, wondering 'who is that woman sitting beside Richard?' Now there really is someone else. She'd heard they'd recently gone to Ibiza. At his age…

When she was a teenager, she had spent a long time like this – this looking in the mirror. 'Who am I?' she'd mouth, watching the reflected lips mouth back. Relieved, then, because 'you must be me.' Then she'd try to fix the face in her mind, so that there would be no more mistaken identity. It didn't work – not with her bare, scrubbed-up features, scraped back hair. But she was a teenager, wasn't she? She could do things to herself. Dye and spike that hair, put a stud in her eyebrow, her lip, her nose; a tattoo on her cheek. A tattoo saying 'This is you!' That would have been useful. Or a 'return to sender' label, so that someone could direct her home, every time she got lost.

It didn't matter, none of it really mattered. She didn't do any of those things. She hardly ever went out. It was too hard.

Lucky, then, to have met Richard, at the one school-dance she did attend. And that, she thought, was that. No need to stand in front of the mirror any more, wondering who she was. She was Richard's wife. Enough.

Now here she is again. Someone. Who?

'Arched, accentuated brows.' She runs her finger around the perfect arcs then touches the brittle, black spiders above her shadowed eyes.

'Green, I think, to match their colour.'

'And bright red on the lips, 'Brilliant Kiss' will do, I think; glittered rouge, on top of the foundation, to heighten your cheek bones.'

She touches the imaginary line, streaking her finger with shimmering dust. Then smears geranium-red from her mouth. It doesn't matter. The lipstick is already spoilt, frayed at the edges, abandoned on three cups of cappuccino.

All this is Jenn, again. Except… it's not. It's her. She had listened to her daughter, her 'have a make-over. It's what everyone does these days, after a divorce', or 'let me do it for you.' So she did. Perhaps the photo on the web-site was a lie, after all.

The thing is… she hadn't liked the look of the other

woman in the café. She doesn't like the look of this woman, now. It's not the make-up, though she thinks it's all too much. Too much, too perfect, not real – though she is someone who has never known what 'real' is. Not even love, as it turned out.

No, what she didn't like then, what she doesn't like now – even more, since she is so close-up, and there can be no denying what she sees… it's the lifeless gaze in the staring eyes, as if, behind the mask, there's nothing there.

She wipes the make-up off. She has these little cotton-wool discs, and a special cream for the task. All these things are new to her, just as the make-up is, all bought for her by Jenn. There seemed no point in lotions and potions before, when her face was a mirage to her. Now, white, fluffy circles, turned the colours of autumn fill the bin. Her face thrown away, all the faces she has ever seen thrown away. All of them, that she can't hold in her mind, from one moment to the next. Groundhog day, everyday. Richard had laughed at that. 'It's the perfect film for you!' he said. A film she might finally be able to watch, because she couldn't watch any others – films or TV programmes. From one scene to the next, she had no idea who the characters were. So yes, Groundhog Day, with its repetition, a day endlessly re-wound, a character stuck in a time-warp, should have made some impact. But it didn't. She may be able to recognise Punxsutawney Phil by his buck-teeth and his fur, but Bill Murray was simply too bland.

Her mother and father, her daughter, the school-friends she never had, her neighbours – they all lie there in the bottom of the bin. Yes, her parents… 'what about them?' the specialist had asked her. 'This kind of thing can be hereditary.' But no, not for her. It was all a mystery, until a childhood accident was remembered; a fall, a knock on the head. 'Ah yes, damage to the FFA, most likely. Only, it hadn't been discovered then. Perhaps you could consider yourself special – in just 1–2 per cent of the population. Although… yours is rather extreme… and coupled with location difficulties. Which does happen.' Lucky her.

The only face that stayed with her was Richard's. Until he walked out.

One last swab of liquid flesh, and there she is. Another face entirely. She thinks. Already the made-up mask has gone from her mind, wiped away into another kind of bin. No. There is no bin, that's the problem. There is no storage area for her to file away the faces she meets… even her own.

There are others, quite the opposite of her, the specialist told her. Those who have super-powers of recognition, who remember every face they've ever seen. And it's all to do with the same part of the brain. 'Amazing!' he said, as if he understood. She tries to imagine what that's like, but can't. Can't because she can't fix one face in her thoughts, let alone thousands. Perhaps it is too much for them. Perhaps they have their problems, too. Perhaps.

So… here she is again, she supposes. There are different lines for her to trace now, real lines, belonging to an old woman. No, not old. Fifty is not old, especially these days – so Jenn keeps telling her. But this face must be older than her teenage self, yet age is something else she cannot fix on. 'It doesn't matter. Age is just a number.' Another of Jenn's lines. If only Richard had felt the same. His new love is twenty years younger, she's been told. If only Richard had been like her.

The carefully-styled hair looks odd against the bare face – it belonged with the powders and creams. She will wash it soon, get rid of that, too, just be whoever she is. This woman, this face, with nothing behind her eyes.

The café with the red geraniums, three to a box, three boxes in a row. She's back again, where she's been day after day, for a few weeks now, waiting for a man who doesn't show. Her own Groundhog Day. Greeting the waiter, ordering her cappuccino, sitting opposite the woman she now knows is her. Or might be. It could be that, some days, they've opened the glass screen, and there is someone else sitting there. Just as the waiter she greets might be a new one each time, who thinks there is something odd about her, because she always asks him 'how are you?' as if they are familiar.

The café is the right one, though, she is sure. There aren't two Russell Streets in the town (she has checked) and the sign is there, up to the left. Anyone else who has visited so often would able to walk to it blindfold by now. But not her.

She is no longer waiting for John, whoever 'John' was. He apologised for missing the last meeting, and said they must re-arrange, but never did, letting their communication falter then fail. Had he turned up that day, she wondered? Stood in a shop doorway opposite, and looked across at the one woman (not two) who sat there? The woman who must be his 'date'. And did he not like what he saw? Not like her face – because that's all he could have seen of her. Judging her on that arrangement of two eyes, a nose, and a mouth.

'Too much make-up,' perhaps he thought, as he turned away. That made her laugh. She is wearing less today. Some, but not as much. She told Jenn she would do it herself this time, because it helped her focus her face – which wasn't true. But, it's better, she thinks.

She moves the cutlery jar forward, then back again. The other woman does the same. So, yes, it must be her. The two of them, sitting there, waiting for the same man.

Peter. It's Peter, this time.

'Well, better than 'John', I suppose,' Jenn says. 'Marginally.'

She is beginning to wish Jenn was not always so ready with her advice. Real Jenn, and the one she carries in her head. She was glad of her in the beginning, it made sense that Jenn knew more about this kind of thing, being younger.

And yet Jenn wasn't really happy about it. 'Why don't you just wait, mum? Wait for someone to come along.' Perhaps that's why she is always so negative. 'Peter' was even better-looking than John, according to Jenn. 'That won't be him,' she said. 'A guy like that would have no trouble getting a young, attractive woman.'

Thank you for that, Jenn.

She has been emailing Peter, back and fore. They seem to have a lot in common. A broken marriage, a love of reading… well, whatever she has mentioned, he has replied the same.

And so, finally, today, they are going to meet. 'Just a coffee, and a chat, to begin with.' She says, Peter says, Jenn says.

'How will you know it's him?' Jenn said, has said from the start. 'You won't know it's the face you've been communicating with.'

'Well, if his photo isn't genuine, he won't look the same, will he? For once, I'll be in the same position as everyone else.' She had liked the thought, even though it had confused her. And Jenn.

'Tell him, mum. Tell him up front.' Something else Jenn said.

But she didn't want to. She knew it would put them off, that she had this 'problem'. That's how they would see it – as a problem, a condition (and yes, it had a Greek name, so that she could make it sound genuine, scientific); or simply something very strange. There was enough to put them off already, with her age, her looks (whatever they were), her boring life.

'Besides, he'll know it's me, even if I don't know it's him. So he'll be the one who comes to sit at my table.'

And, besides, I'm usually the only person there, she didn't add. The one woman… or two.

Still, she thought of telling him to wear a red carnation, as people used to do, on such occasions, before social media made it all so much more… 'accessible'. Carnation, not geranium. Even these geraniums are not perky enough to put in a button-hole. Still, she hasn't seen a red carnation for a while now. 'Do they still 'make' them?' The mouth of the woman opposite gapes up and down, along with her throat. She's doing this more often, lately. Saying her thoughts/ Jenn's thoughts, whoever's thought, out loud. It must stop, it has to stop. Something else 'not right' with her, to add to all her other imperfections. But where is he? Why doesn't he come? Whoever he is…

And an hour later, he's still not there. She gets up, her other self gets up, and together they head home.

John, Peter, Philip, Malcolm. The men change, the months go by, along with the visits to the café. The geraniums die and get replaced with miniature conifers, and trailing ivy – not so easy for her to latch on to, but there's that 'Russell Street' sign, still up there on the left. She has to sit inside now.

Philip turned up, but made excuses afterwards. Malcolm was a 'no-show', like the first two.

Richard got married last week. The baby's due in a couple of months. Jenn's thrilled to be having a new baby half-brother/sister.

Today, she's waiting for Charles.

A man walks across the street, a man with no distinguishing features (she's still going for that look, though she really should give up on it), so it might be him. He's not wearing a red carnation, but she never asked him to. Besides, he probably couldn't get one. He's coming towards her, smiling. The woman opposite rises from her seat. Perhaps she's been waiting for him, too. Which is he going to pick, she wonders? Me? No, me.

'Charles?' she says. 'Yes,' he replies. So it must be him. Mustn't it?

Hello, hello. He doesn't say her name in return, so she says it. 'Helen.'

'Of course.' Of course, she is Helen. Who else would she be? And he sits down with her, and smiles.

I'm leaving the café with the red geraniums, which are no longer there, which have magicked themselves into imitation Christmas trees, minus the decorations. I'm leaving with Charles. The waiter winks at me, as Charles pays the bill. 'At last!' he's probably thinking. 'Finally' – if, of course, he's the same one who's served me so many times before. I've really no idea.

Charles is taking me to a restaurant 'a little place he knows'. We're not going round the corner from Russell Street, towards the library, along from the station. He's taking me in the other direction, down a short-cut by the canal. I've lived in this town all my life, but I have no idea if this is the right way to go – I haven't a clue where we're going, after all. Jenn would say I shouldn't be doing this, not 'first date'. 'Always have other people around you. Always make sure someone knows where you are going. Never be alone in a lonely place.'

But I'm not alone. The other woman is coming with me. I can see her now, in the windows of the deserted buildings lining the tow-path. She's smiling, smiling, just like I am, her lips stretched, her gums showing. But she still has that dead look behind her eyes.

In the Warehouse of the Unloved Dead…

After dark, in the warehouse of the unloved dead, Hamer sidles through the shadows beneath the matchbox catacombs. He knows where to go – the beam of his torch illuminates the crosses he has etched in the dust-shrouds, leading him on. His own version of a trail of breadcrumbs, or a hero's thread. At last, he reaches his destination, in the furthermost reaches of the black cavern. Here, Robert Dukowsky lies beneath Miss Clara Waite, who is to the left of Miriam Samuel, who is above Mr. Morgan Duff… who is next to Robert Dukowsky. An outcrop in the wall of earthly remains stretching back, back all the way he has come, and up, up, to an unseen heaven.

He touches the box closest to him, in greeting. Morgan Duff. He likes this. He likes to think how 'death is the great leveller', as the saying goes; how, in death, you find the most unlikely bedfellows. What would the rich, cultured Mr Robert Dukowsky think if he knew he had been placed next to the scoundrel, Duff?

And Hamer eases into the chair he has placed in the corner, and smiles.

Tonight, he will begin with Robert. It will be the Duke's turn to have the casket holding all that is left of him opened and rummaged through.

'You mean… You see their bones… or anything else that's left of them… their decomposing… flesh!'

There is Nell, sitting opposite him in the restaurant booth, on their first date; her eyes and nose scrunched, her lips twisting. Her fork, tipped with a thread of bloody steak, sags towards her plate.

She had got it all wrong, of course. But it was his fault.

He had misled her when they first met, same as he did with everyone back then. It took no more than a slipped word or two, a rush of breath through his teeth, or a shake of the head. That's all.

'New job,' he said to Bea, his coffee girl. 'A caretaker in a storage…'

The screaming whoosh of the machine evaporated his words. Her smile was as fixed as the clover in the froth of his cappuccino.

'In a place down town,' he told Fred, his neighbour. 'Huge place. You can't imagine it. For all these boxes…'

'Gotta go,' Fred interrupted. 'Dinner's about done.'

Then he found if you got 'dead' in early on, their eyes snapped away from machines and meal-times, and fixed on him, instead.

They would *listen*. That's all he wanted.

And he knew, by then, that such places existed. Huge underground chambers, layer upon layer of corpses, packed tight as his favourite triple-decker club. And some had been turned into museums, in Rome, Paris, places like that. So why not here? Why couldn't he be some kind of attendant, in charge of mouldering skulls and jumbled bones, showing people around the place from time to time, pointing out who lay where? Instead of a man spending his days sitting amongst wooden crates, full of *stuff*.

Of course, he'd had to change the story with Nell pretty quick, because he already knew he wanted to get serious with her. All that talk about death was okay for your pass-the-time-of-day acquaintances, but not so good with the person you'd decided you wanted to spend the rest of your life with, by first-date dessert. Lying wasn't so good, in fact.

'Get it said, Hamer,' he told himself. 'Get it said about how boring it can be, sitting there day after day, amongst all those boxes, hardly anyone ever coming by.'

But she'd found it interesting, when he explained what

the crates held.

'Never heard of such a thing! Never thought about it before! All those 'worldly goods' being kept by the State, for a 'decent amount of time', looked after by you. That's quite a responsibility you got there.'

By then, he liked to think much the same. Skeletons – even those with gobbets of flesh still clinging on – what did they mean? Nothing. Well, maybe, perhaps, if you were a forensic M.E., wanting to know how someone had died. Or an archaeologist trying to discover how people had lived. But you could do all that with their belongings, too. In fact, you could do it *more*. What they bought, what they kept around them, shared their space with, right till the moment they passed on – those could tell you everything you needed to know about a person. And there he was, in his job, a custodian of their life stories, preserving them, because there was no-one else to do it, just like there was no-one for them to leave their possessions to.

'Who've you got in your life?' Nell asked him, at the end of that first meal. 'Nobody. Nobody at all,' he replied, 'though I'm hoping that might change real soon!'

The Duke, the Duke, focus on the Duke. 'Forget about Nell, forget about everyone else. Nothing else matters, now. Just this.'

The Duke's is the biggest crate – well, not 'biggest crate', exactly, because all the outer shells are the same size, for easy stacking. But the Duke's own personal inner box is the biggest Hamer's come across. Not that he knows them all, of course; there are far too many for that. Sad, so sad, all these lonely people dying without a single heir. You'd think it would be possible to find one, just one, no matter how distant. Not that he agrees with any old second-cousin-twice-removed getting your things; he thinks it's right there's a point when 'family' is cut off. Even so, there are still plenty of options for 'next of kin'. He knows them all; recites 'the order of inheritance' to himself, when he's having trouble sleeping, his own insomniac's mantra.

'Spouse' (shame it begins with 'spouse', rubbing salt in the wound, reminding him of Nell, which isn't the best idea, when he's trying to get to sleep. But there it is.)

Spouse.

Children.

Parents.

Siblings.

On and on down to

great-great-grandchildren/parents/nieces-nephews.

At least a couple of dozen chances of having some relative stashed away somewhere under a stone, waiting to jump out at the possibility of a hand-me-down from someone they've never met.

Except here he is, a living example of how easy it is to lose them all – or simply not have them in the first place.

Sure, he'd had a mother – everyone had to have a mother, even if only for the nine months of carrying, and the few minutes of birth. ('Few minutes!?' he remembered her saying to him once. 'Few days, more like. God, what I went through for you!') Minutes, days – well, he'd had his a while longer than that, until his twenties, in fact. But he'd never felt close to her. And yet he should have; all they had was each other. When he was a kid, he couldn't understand how the other neighbourhood children had all these brothers, sisters, cousins, uncles and aunts, gathering around for barbecues in the yard, or great-grandma Susan's hundredth birthday.

'I'm an only child,' she'd say. 'Your grandparents died in a car crash. They didn't have anyone, either. So that's it. Just you and me, babe.'

'What about my Dad?' But who his father was seemed as insubstantial as all those missing relatives.

'Forget him. He doesn't exist.'

But he must have once, if only for the briefest of moments.

The Duke. Mr. Robert Dukowsky. 'Get on with it, Hamer.' An immigrant from eastern Europe, surely. An immigrant made good.

Mr Robert Dukowsky walks along the street, hat on head, cane in hand, waistcoat with gold watch-chain peeping through. He nods – almost a small bow – to everyone he meets, but he knows no-one. The only people he has contact with are the workers in the bank he runs – runs successfully, runs well. Which is why Mr. Robert Dukowsky has so much money, to spend on the things he likes. Books, more gold jewellery, paintings, fine clothes; more books, more gold, more paintings. Dukowsky is most definitely a collector. First editions, a particular artist, coins, stamps. The kind of person for whom the searching of a special something is like a chase, followed by that feeling of victory, when you bring it home. All these things he's acquired – they are there waiting for him, when he gets in from the office, waiting for him to roll on his soft, white gloves, to turn a single page, or tweezer another stamp into black paper corners. They keep him company into the long, late hours. Because there's no-one else around.

Dukowsky, reaching the corner, nods to Miss Clara Waite. Not that he knows that she is Miss Clara Waite. He simply sees a small, bent woman, with a perpetual half-smile on her lips, and wide, flitting eyes. She scurries past, with no acknowledgement. It is better not to respond to any overtures of communication, even if they come from respectable-looking gentlemen – yes, he is surely a gentleman. But, still, he is a stranger. You never know. Better to get home quickly, and bolt the door, and make a cup of tea, a habit she acquired on her trip to England, and tell Dolly all about it – how she was virtually accosted in the street by a strange man.

Miss Clara Waite is not alone. She has Dolly to talk to. And Princess, and May-belle, and… Her cats; her cats of the moment. There are always cats in Clara's apartment, in her life; live cats… dead cats. Because, when one of her cats dies, Clara likes to have it stuffed. She knows a good man she found from a store advert. He does the best job, the most amazing job. You'd never guess… if it wasn't for the lack of movement, the twitch of a nose, the heave of a purr. It's as if... they never leave her. Trixie, Merry, Fluff – they're always still there.

And they're still here, too. Shut away in Miss Waite's box, shut away for now, but Hamer's seen them often enough. And yes, they're still in half-way good condition – you've got to give the taxidermist guy credit for that – just a little tear in Puss's ear, a mite of fraying on Apple's rump, but really, not too bad on the whole.

One time… one time when he was feeling particularly low, he found himself stroking one of them. It felt good, the smooth rub beneath his palm, the rhythmic back and fore. He'd heard that about cats – how they could be a comfort. Though he reckoned that was live ones, not dead. Not stuffed.

It was soon after Nell had left. He had done a lot of strange things, then.

Nell liked the story of the cats. 'You're kidding me!' she'd said, when he first told her. 'Twenty-seven of the things! Oh my… imagine being told you'd inherited after some distant relative, then turning up to find twenty-seven stuffed cats! Mind, you gotta feel for Miss Clara – poor woman!'

'Poor cats, I'd say…'

'Oh, I don't know… if she took good care of them…'

And she did, he knows that. He knows it from their velvet collars, with the silver name tags, that still hang around their stuffed necks; from their fine-china feeding bowls, and grooming tools, top-of-the-range kitty beds, and scratching-posts.

'The only things she had left belonged to her cats?'

'Well, yes…'

'Like I said – poor woman.'

And yes, she is. Anyone who ends up in here has to be pitiful, don't they?

Like him… There, he's thinking about Nell again. 'Get a grip, Hamer, get a grip.' It's what happens, though, isn't it? The love of your life… you never can help the way they stay with you, just lurking around in the back of your mind most of the time, then jumping out 'surprise', whenever something brings you down. He rubs his hand across the top of his thigh. The pocket crackles beneath it. Yes, the letter's still there, where he pushed it this morning.

Miss Clara has a letter, too. Funny, but he never told Nell about it, about the letter, and the plane ticket for England, and the hotel bill, and the postcards of bright red buses and Big Ben and St. Paul's – all tied up with a pink ribbon, in a carved, mother-of-pearl-inlay miniature chest. The words on the tissue-thin blue paper are hard to make out in some places, washed by tears, he's sure, but he can still read 'sorry/a mistake/goodbye', and really, you don't need to know more.

You don't even need to know that, sometimes. You don't even need to have those few words. There was no note when Nell left, but he knew it as soon as he'd got home. Knew it from the empty space where his car was parked, followed by the half-open door. Funny, not for a moment did he think 'thieves/muggers/murderers!' He just felt it straight away, as if he could taste the empty air, as if this was always going to happen. Of course, she hadn't bothered to shut the door, because there was nothing left worth stealing inside – there had never been much, but she'd taken anything worth half a buck with her, along with all her own things.

And who, by then, was he to judge?

Hamer shrugs himself up from the floor, where he's been crouched amongst the Duke's belongings. His knees are getting too old for this; all of him's getting too old for this. The Duke's gold fob-watch weighs heavy in his hand. 'Good morning, Miss Waite, four minutes to eleven, precisely,' Robert would say to Clara, when she stopped to ask him the time. Except she never did. Foolish Clara, who knows what might have happened if she had? Or perhaps she was right to keep silent, knowing by then, the hurt love could bring you.

He'd stolen for Nell. He'd never done it for himself, no matter that he already knew how much valuable stuff lay all around him, easy pickings for someone with a crow-bar and an access-code.

Yes, she'd laughed at the story of Miss Clara Waite's cats, but it was Mr. Robert Dukowsky she was more interested in.

'All that jewellery and fancy goods, just shut away, waiting for the State to get its grubby hands on it. Doesn't seem right, does it?'

'Well, sometimes the State puts it to good use, and you never know… some kin may still turn up and claim it.'

'Yeh, like what? Some fifth-down-the-line, three across, never even met the guy types? Why should they get it? Besides, you said yourself only one genuine claimant had turned up, in all the time you've been there.'

'I guess…'

And he wanted to give her things. It seemed to matter. The way she looked after he had presented her with some little gift, something pretty and shiny. She lit up, which made him light up. That's all it was. So he kidded himself that she was right, that it wasn't really stealing. Okay, so he was depriving the State of some small amount of money, but it was arguable that it was theirs in the first place – well, it wasn't. It belonged to whoever had accumulated it throughout their lives. Like Robert. And who was the only person on the planet who gave Robert a thought? Him. A kind thought, at that.

And he never took anything too much. Not at first. Only, when he saw how pleased Nell was by the little things, he found himself wanting to give her bigger things. It seemed to make her happier, happier with him, especially when she'd been glum for a while. She might even say 'why don't you give me nothing no more?' So then he would take something, something bigger, better, shinier, and present it to her, and she would smile, and be good to him that night.

So who was he to blame her – that she'd taken it all when she left, and all the cash she knew he kept in his bedside drawer, and his medals, and his sports' trophies? Who was he to call her 'thief'?

But he hadn't given her the watch. It was Dukowsky's, and only his. 'To Robert, with love from Helen, always.' Another what-might-have-been, to go along with Clara's English beau. Another opportunity for staying out of this place lost. Like him with Nell…

Perhaps he'll just rest his eyes for a while, have a nap, even, before...

Why not? He does it most nights now, ever since he took to coming back after dark. He's more likely to sleep here than in his cold, lonely bed.

'God, it must be quiet in there!' Nell had said to him.

'Well, you'd be surprised!'

It was another of his jokes, when he was fooling around about working with the dead. 'Sometimes… well, sometimes, you might think there's someone in there still alive. The sounds you hear!'

He'd been surprised, too, in his first months there. Music! That had been the strangest! A ground-out up-and-down kind of tune. A music-box, he'd figured in the end. Another old-maid's fondest possession, reminding her of her one-and-only dance, her imagined love. On and on it went, and there was nothing he could do, just wait till it wound itself down.

Same with the clock – another thing his ears had latched on to, one time. Tick-tock, tick-tock, deep in the belly of the place – strange, how it wasn't there, then was, in a crate that must have been deposited years ago. Could clocks start up again, he wondered? Was it battery, or clockwork – and which would run out first? He thought it would drive him mad, and there were times when he was half-asleep, when it sounded like the faint throbbing of a steady pulse, so he could almost believe the stories he told others.

'You'd swear you could hear breathing,' he'd tell his open-mouthed listeners. 'Or sighing…' That was when there was a settling in the contents of a new arrival, or a creaking in the wood of a long-time occupant. 'You wonder, then, what if there's anyone down there still alive? Crazy, I guess. But ghosts, maybe?'

'Do they wail? Like in the movies?' Maeve at the deli check-out asked him. 'Or whooo-whooo like in Scooby Doo?'

Perhaps, by then, people didn't take his stories seriously any more. Perhaps he'd gone too far with them.

But weren't they a kind of ghost, after all? The shadowy remains of a person – wasn't that what a ghost was?

They're quiet, now; the sounds he hears are of a different kind, as the other creatures of the night come alive. The scritch-scratch of beetles, as they begin their nightly rounds. Beetles are levellers, too. They'll enter any crate, high or low, get through any crack, crevice or cranny. Eat anything. He's read up on beetles – how many different kinds there are, the type of damage they can do. The worm-holes in Robert's books are most likely caused by the larder beetle (dermestes lardarius); they like the leather. He knows Robert wouldn't be pleased.

Then there's moth – you have to strain your ears real hard to pick up on that tiny breath of air. But he knows they're there. It's moth that's responsible for the gap in Puss's ear.

Or him… what if it's his fault? What if it's because he opens these crates? They're not supposed to be opened, after all. Perhaps all the others are fine – he's only seen one other open. That was after some State official appeared, saying an alleged spouse had turned up, and they were after some kind of evidence of her existence. They didn't find anything. 'Didn't expect to,' the guy said to him. 'We're pretty sure she's just trying it on. That's women for you.'

'Oh, I don't know…'

That was when he and Nell were still together, when he thought he was going to have a spouse – a genuine, loving, 'till death us do part' kind of person. He was going to have someone, anyone. Well, not just anyone. The 'spouse' was the top of the list, the first in the line, your absolute next of kin, the closest to you. But there was something else about a spouse – a 'wife', as it was, in the case of a man. They could give you children.

'Have you ever thought about children?' he'd asked her once. She'd just laughed. But he had begun dreaming. He had thought he was past all that, but she was that much younger than him. There could be one, even two, perhaps, a boy and a girl. A boy who looked like him, a girl pretty like her mother. He could see them! A family… the family he'd never had before. All that would happen when she married him.

Another couple of weeks, and he was going to ask her. Another couple of pay-packets, to pay for the ring he wanted to buy her. Another wad of notes in his bedside drawer for her to take away with her.

That was when he started coming here nighttimes, or not going home at all. Just slipping out for a quick bite, then coming back in. The ghosts – those shadowy remains – he'd made them into something far more, by then. Added flesh to their bones, substance to their spirits – least he had with these four, closest to him. Given them faces, gestures; feelings, even.

So that it wasn't only stroking a stuffed cat that gave him comfort. He had company! He had people to talk to. People who didn't roll their eyes heaven-ward, when he spoke about himself. People who didn't make you fall in love with them, then disappear, robbing you blind. Even Morgan Duff wouldn't do that, would he? Well, maybe…

And now… and now…

Hamer pulls the letter from his pocket, smoothes it on his thigh.

'Read it,' the Duke tells him.

'I know what it says.'

He knows the words that matter. 'Terminate/employment/notice'. He's too old for this now, apparently. And there have been certain complaints.

'What are you going to do, after you leave here? You're like us – you've got no-one else. You haven't even got *things*. You borrow my books, Clara's cats, even; Morgan's…'

It was true. What Nell had taken… it was the best of him, you might say. She left him with nothing, and he was nothing. And it was too late to put something new in its place – what would be the point? So what he had now, bar the clothes and furniture he'd taken to the thrift shop, fitted into a large holdall. He'd brought it with him tonight.

'Get on with it,' Morgan chips in. 'Even if those suckers don't know what you've got planned, I sure do.'

He had made a fire after his mother died. You could say she was a collector, like Robert – every room of her house rammed full of … stuff. 'Hoarder' might be a better word, though. You could be a hoarder, even if there was nothing worth hoarding. Newspapers and magazines tied in string bundles, piled to the ceiling, and yet he had never seen her read a paper in her life! Turned out she got them from a neighbour, who thought he was doing her a favour, by passing them on. Clothes, shoes, bulging out of cupboards and drawers, draped on the chairs – all different sizes, in styles going back years. But she never went anywhere! So why did she buy them, let alone keep them? And most of them were full of moth holes, or daubed in mould, too bad to go back to the thrift shops they'd come from in the first place. Food-packaging – he couldn't get his head round that one at all. Rubbish, trash, junk – all of it – nothing but. 'One man's trash is another man's treasure,' the newspaper neighbour said. But no, not with this.

He'd taken the stuff outside, piled it high, and set a match to it. It was the right thing to do. Otherwise, it would have gone into land-fill. He wondered if people knew enough about landfill, really thought about it, how there was far too much waste, clogging up the planet. Far better to burn it, though the stack was slow to catch, on account of being damp, but it flared in the end. Flared, then dwindled to ash, the same as she was now. All that was left… except for him, and look where that had got to. No-one. Nothing.

The damp won't be a problem here, not with the carefully monitored temperature thermostat gauge.

'My books…' he can hear Robert saying. 'My beautiful possessions…'

'You should have married Helen.'

'You don't know…'

'But I do, I do.'

'You have no idea…'

'Or at least left them to a library, a museum, have them put to some use. And they'd have put your name on the label – 'donated by' – so you wouldn't be forgotten. A plaque, even. Or was it that you didn't want anyone else to have them? Even though, as you now know, if you didn't before, you can't take it with you!'

'I didn't know I was going to die. I thought I had years left. I still…'

'My cats!' Clara's joining in, now.

The cats will burn easily, he imagines. They'll help things get going, spread.

'You should never have had them. If you hadn't had them to talk to, perhaps you'd have answered Robert, when he greeted you, and who knows where that might have led? And what about the baby? Your baby?'

Something else in Clara's box, beneath the letter and souvenirs – a tiny, soft-toy rabbit, dressed in pink, 'Your baby's first cuddle!', along with an adoption certificate. 'You should have kept her! You should never have given her away!'

'You don't understand! Times were…'

'And then you would have had someone, instead of just a bunch of cats; a child to stop you ending up in here!'

'And what about you?' Morgan, of course. 'What about your father? He might still be out there, mightn't he? Might not be that old, if he was just a kid when he had that roll in the hay. You never tried, did you? Never tried to find him.'

'I…'

'Still, you're right enough about the cats. It's time they went. Lived, stuffed, stuck in a box, waiting to be eaten away bit by bit. They'll be glad to finally get it over with. Talking of which…'

In the warehouse of the unloved dead, Hamer lies down beneath the matchbox catacombs. He fits himself in between Robert Dukowsky, Miss Clara Waite, Morgan Duff, and Miriam Samuel.

There will be a real dead body in here now – he likes the thought. All those things he fooled people with – bones, flesh, lying around the place – it will be true… depending on how much gets left after burning. Maybe there'll be nothing left but ash. Like with his mother – her body, and her things. 'It's what they should have done with it all in the first place,' Miriam Samuel whispers. Miriam, who he's never been able to get a word out of before. Miriam, who came over here, after surviving the Holocaust; who knows more than any about losing everything, including all your family; who knows more than any about how things burn.

‘There’s a saying ‘you come in to the world with nothing, you leave it with nothing’. But nobody wants it to be true these days, do they?’

Hamer closes his eyes, and smiles.

Rules for Going Skipping

I'm putting the baby back in the skip tonight – the one I found last week. It's better this way, with things not working out like they ought. Guess I shoulda left her where she was.

Didn't see her, first skim through – reckon my 'skip eyes' were still half-shut. Not till I'd jumped right in and yanked a square of carpet, high enough to make my teeth water. 'Dog,' I was thinking, '… could be worse.'

Her basket lay between a still-boxed slo-cooker and a wheezing gas-bottle – something else that shouldn't have been there. Gas bottles, fridges, asbestos, batteries… needles, definitely not needles! – I have a list in my head of *Authority's Prohibited items for disposal*. 'Babies' isn't on it.

'Pixie! Get out of there!' It's always Elsa who's bugging me, unless it's Mollie, with the gang's own *Rules appertaining to the removal of objects from other people's removable recycling facilities* – or something like that. Another list I'm sposed to keep in my head.

'How else you gonna to find the best things?' I asked the first time she found me knee-deep in a fifteen yard roll-on, roll-off, straddling a stack of tyres (not allowed) and a moth-grazed moose-head (permitted). Now, just think they're all plain jealous, being too lardy and long-toothed to climb in and out.

Just like I sussed they made up half these rules to suit their hoiting-toiting selves. Take their rule Number Three – *Always scrub your hands thoroughly after a morning's work.*

'Wash your hands, Pixie, for goodness sake!'

'Better still, wear gloves. It's so much more hygienic!'

'Wash before we have a cup of tea, Pixie!' 'Oh…'

Wash, full stop, is what they want to say. Their noses scrunkle up whenever I'm near, like some fretful weevil grub, or a scenting badger.

Funny to mind the niff of a person, when you fritter your

free time scrummaging in other folk's waste. Dirt is good, they should know.

'Gotta ha' your peck of it,' one of my dads used to say, every time he shooed us out the door.

I guess he was right enough, 'bout that, if not much else.

I've put her back in the basket, now, all ready to take, all swaddled up tight like a baby Jesus, just like when I found her; all quiet and unmoving, so that I thought I was seeing a doll (those bleary skip-eyes again), until she scrunched up her little face. 'BABY!' There it was, coming from inside my head and heading loud outta my gawping lips, only I snatched it back just in time. Phew! I knew, if I said it, there'd be trouble, that even though it wasn't on the 'forbidden items' list, there'd be a subsection about babies in there somewhere. *If a baby is found in a skip, the Authorities must be informed straight away.* Or something like that. Another rule. There sure are plenty of them, what with Authority's and our own. Plenty if you're hiring a skip, plenty more if you're going through them. All these dos and don'ts. All these things you've got to do, you're not to do, you mustn't do, you shouldn't do. Do this Pixie, do that. Don't Pixie, don't do that. No, Pixie, no. NNOOOO!

'YOU CAN'T PLAY!' I'm just hanging on for Elsa to say it, like the girls in the school yard used. 'Go away, Pixie!' 'Get lost, just get lost!'

'Apples, peaches, pears and plums, tell me when your birthday comes.' Not you, Pixie, not you.

'I like coffee, I like tea, I like Lizzie, Holly, Suzy, to jump with me.' Anyone but Pixie.

Can't play hopscotch, can't play 'catch'. Can't share my sweets. Can't come to my party. Can't have a go. Can't play skipping… until now.

Until Judy knocked at my door, and said 'Do you want to come skipping with us, Pixie?' So that, there we'd be, I figured, grown women, hand in hand, lolopping down the street, or twirling rope in the park, and 'me' being allowed to jump in for the first time in my life. Me telling when my birthday is. '5th of May! I know that. I do know it!' And Judy must have seen my foolish notions in my face, cos she burst out laughing and said, 'no, not that! Going through skips, and rescuing other people's cast-offs and turning them into something nice.'

I guess that's what I thought I'd do with the baby.

Three, six, nine. Da da, da da.

Clap, clap. Clap, clap. I still like to sing the skipping songs, when we go 'skipping', even though it's not the right kind. Makes me feel kind of … belonged. 'Rule four, five, six and seven/Dive right in, and go to heaven!' That's one of my own… Clap, clap.

'Found anything, Pix?' And there was Judy, sashaying over to me, all smiles and nice-nice, cos that's how Judy is.

'Nope,' I said, and clambered out, quick as a spooked rat. 'I guess the skip fairy's not with me today!'

Rule number one, *You must have the skip fairy with you to find something worth retrieving*. Sometimes I fancy these women are crazier than me. I'm the one called Pixie, and they're the ones who believe in fairies… skip fairies, leastwise.

'Not even a doll?' If that had been Elsa, I'd be sure she was having a go. They know how mad I am about dolls. That every time I found one, I'd be jumping up and down, punching the air, and 'YAYing' way too loud. And then, there they'd be with their eyebrows pushing up to their hairlines, and their huffing, strong enough to send any stray bits of newspaper furling down the street, with them chasing after – ha ha to that! Before they'd be saying, 'Pixie, and her dolls again!'

And yes, I guess I got too many – all a-looking down at me and the baby from shelves, and cupboards, and window-ledges, anyways they can fit – too crammed for a caravan, it's true. And yes, I sure don't mind whatever state they're in, cos it's a funny thing with dolls, how they can be so loved, and get so messed up all the same. Too much bathing, cradling, fussing – loved to bits, you might say. But then, there's the hate side, with sisters fighting, hell-for-leather, hair-pulling, nails a-scratching, and the doll gets in between; or brothers getting their own back for tales told… it's something boys do. They don't like being told on. Boys, or even grown men. They don't like it at all.

Take Lucy, hooked on the curtain rail, who came from a skip on Dewberry Road with an arm and leg long gone. Well, that's not the Worst Thing in the World, cos you can take the lost limbs off another poor lamb who's past all hope, and push them on in. Some might consider she looks kinda strange, with one fat leg, and one thin, and one pink arm, and one peachy, but not me. Or there's Martha, perched on the fridge… no eyes when I found her. I'm betting on a grinning brother there, sticking a scissors in the sockets and squeezing them out. I've put blue beads instead. She looks okay, though a bit goggle-eyed, in the dusk-light, when I've lit the lamp, when she follows me round with her rabbit-caught-in-the-headlights stare. But I don't mind. The others snigger behind their hands, and won't put them up for sale in their car-boots, and craft-fayres, and pop-up shops, but suits me. Don't want to sell them, anyway. I want to keep them every single one, all my baby dolls most of all, cos they're my favourites, cos you can hold them tight, to your chest, and rock them back and fore in your arms, and feel all gooey inside. Kinda warm. Rosa was my favourite of all, being one of those all-singing, all-dancing real-life types. The kind little girls have to practise for the real thing. The kind my mother shoulda had but didn't. I kept her in bed beside me, and cuddled her all the time. Until I brought the baby home, and then I cuddled her instead.

'Never mind,' Judy said, 'come and see what we've

found.' So I scurried over to where they were all chummied up together further down the road, like a gaggle of yakking hens, disobeying the rule of working in pairs. There they were, ohhing and ahhing over a zinc bath with only one small hole in it, that would surely fetch five pounds in a boot-sale, more, if it got painted and filled with marigolds and lobelia. Plus a chair with just one broke leg, and only a teensy bit of its rush seat missing. So I ohhed and ahhed too, fingers and everything else crossed that the baby wouldn't start wailing. Otherwise, it would be 'game up' and all that police/fire/ambulance panic – or, leastwise, they were surely going to have to ask the skip-owner about it… something else I don't get ever. Rule number two. *Always ask permission from the skip-hirer, also known as the owner of the discarded rubbish, usually located in the nearest available dwelling*. I mean, if you put something in a skip, you're throwing it away. Right? You don't want it any more. Isn't that the plan? So why would you be bothered if someone else could find a use for it? A bit more space in your precious cubic inches, after all. *(Never overfill your skip, or it may result in failure of taking it away!)* But there you go, there they are every time we go out, knocking at doors, till they get the right one. 'Would you mind...?' 'Please could I...?' 'Oh, thank you so much. How kind, so very, very kind!'

Some days, by the time they've done all that smarmy simpering, I've already got the best bits out and ferreted them down in the *Additional space allowance of five feet behind the next vehicle to allow room to position the container.* And sometimes, from where I'm peeking, I see the owner's squirms and stutters, like they don't want anyone to know about the stuff they've thrown in there. All those things on the forbidden list they tucked away at the bottom – that bit of asbestos from their old shed. All their light bulbs and batteries, which have their own special section in the council recycling facility, if only you can be bothered to get there. And even with the permitted items, it's 'how did so very nice, middle-class me, buy that awful wicker chair, and now this woman's seen it, and seen the state I've kept it in?' Which is how I reckoned it was with the one-legged chair on this particular day…

Least I figured it wasn't Mrs. Perfect in Number Five (she of the broken chair), who put the baby in the skip, even if it was six houses along from hers. Because that would be just stupid, wouldn't it? That's the kind of thing you do from much further away. Covering your tracks, you might say. Not that you're supposed to put your throw-aways in another person's skip – babies, or anything else. Putting things in, taking things out – *Only those who have paid the hiring fee, have any rights over the contents of the receptacle.*

So then it was phone Mollie's sister, to come over with the car. Because that's rule number four – *Always have a vehicle on standby, in the event of larger items necessitating removal.*

And then off we went, another day's skipping over. But not for me.

I'm waiting till it's dark to take Jane back. Like I dawdled round till midnight to go back and fetch her. Sure enough, I've given her a name, like I name all the dolls. A nice, ordinary name, I like to think. Not like Pixie, or Starlight, my mother, though she wasn't always called that, Judy tells me. Judy tells me lots of things about my mother, they being friends once upon a time. That's why she lets me live on her place – though not too close, of course. That's why she's kind to me.

No, Jane's better. And 'better' is what I was after. Better than how it was for me. Which wouldn't take much, truth be told. Better than all my brothers and sisters. Better than the kids in foster homes. Or just 'Homes'. Better than being left in a skip, anyways. Which wouldn't take much, either.

'Who would do that?' I was wondering, as I scooted through the wood, past Judy's front door, and back into town. But then, who would throw away that slo-cooker? Put a rabbit-stew on before you go out, nice and piping for you when you come back. Who wouldn't want that? And who wouldn't have wanted Lucy? I saw the girl who threw her out – least I think I did. Hanging round the front door, talking on her mobile, flicking back her hair, pouting her lips. Too old for a doll now, is what she thought. Boys were the new toys. Someone should tell her dolls are safer.

But, of course, when it's a baby, hundred-and-ten per cent it's the mother who's done the throwing – a desperate mother. It's only when you're feeling real bad you do something like that. That's what Starlight always told me, whenever she sent me away, whenever she put the needle into her arm again.

Course, I found the skip easy enough, with its lights blaring and reflective strips reflecting away. 'What if it's gone?' nagged at me, as I shimmied in. 'What if the mother's had second-thoughts, or Mrs. Perfect's found it?'… But no, it was still there, hidden beneath another piss-steeped slice of Axminster. Lucky it wasn't anything harder, lucky it was summer. Lucky, lots of things, cos a skip's not the Best Place in the World to leave a baby, no matter how low you're feeling. There's so many bad things could happen. That gas bottle, for instance. Boom! Or some passing junkie might toss a hypo in, even though he's not allowed, they're not allowed – shouldn't be allowed anywhere, is what I think, but specially near babies, in or out the womb. Still, it can be the same anywhere, I'm reckoning. A cottage in a wood. Those children's homes. In care – it's a funny word, care. So many ways to hurt a baby, in or out of a skip, before or after it's born. And you can still hurt it, when it's almost grown up. I know that for a fact.

And so I grabbed the basket, and lugged it home, without much looking. Put it on the bed, and pulled it out, no more than a bundle of rags. One sheet after the other, like some kind of shroud. Or a children's pass the parcel game – not that I ever played one of those, either. Kept on thinking I would hit blue or pink, a kitted out fully paid-up baby, with a note attached of the 'please look after my child' variety, plus a bottle with some feed, and a change, I was hoping. But there was nothing. Just a scrap of a baby.

A girl… and then there was sad Pixie and glad Pixie squabbling inside. Thinking it was a girl I was really after, remembering from BEFORE; but thinking, too, that girls had it tougher than boys, with even more C.R.A.P. hanging over them – least that's how it seemed to me. But still, all my dolls were girls. So I guess in the end, happy Pixie won. Until I looked at her and saw how scrawny she was. Okay. Babies are small, specially before they're born. I know that. I know how tiny a baby inside can be, how weak. How easy to harm. But they're sposed to be bigger when they get birthed. Only, Jane was smaller than Rosa even. And where was the crying? Crying is what babies do, even if I didn't want it, even though people don't hear crying in a wood. Another thing I know for a fact. But Judy might come calling, so a quiet baby would suit me fine. But not this quiet. Nothing but this thin mew now and then, getting fainter and fainter, with each hour that passed.

Still…but… there was me, still determined. 'I can do this! I can take care of this child, small or not, quiet or not. I can, I can!'

And I tried! I tried! Sunday, Monday, Tuesday, Wednesday. Lord knows how I tried!

'It's not as if I don't know how to look after a baby!' That's what I told the women from Authority before! When they came knocking with their belted macks, high heels and black briefcases. 'It's not the same as looking after a doll,' is what they told me back. I know that! I knew it then. But they wouldn't listen. They just took her out the door!

And 'like mother, like daughter', is what they said, next time round. As if, somehow, there were no fathers involved. As if I was like Starlight, but I wasn't! 'I'm not,' I screamed. 'I'm not!'

'I'm clean!' I shouted. Meaning, not the opposite of 'dirty' kind of clean, – I hold my grubby paws up to that! But 'clean' of the other variety… 'I'm clean! I always have been. Okay, maybe back at the very beginning, when I was still in the womb, but that wasn't my doing!'

But 'better safe than sorry,' is what they said. 'Please,' I said back. 'Please.' Again and again.

But it was no good.

So third time lucky. And fingers crossed, skip fairy sprinkling magic dust and all that, is what I've been hoping. Together with figuring 'things are better now, with my little caravan, and an 'outside interest', and no Starlight around, doing up or chasing dragons in the corner'. Besides, I've got all the rules in my head, for *What to do with items you find in a skip, and how to make them better*. Rules one to ten, or however many there are. I've been going over every single means of *Upcycling*, as they like to call it, of turning *Trash found in a skip into treasure*! Determined to make it better than Judy's 'retro' oil-can table lamp, complete with patchwork shade, or Mollie's 'vintage' garden ornament made out of only slightly chipped flowerpots. Or even that wall-eyed, mangy moose head of Elsa's (nicked from under my nose – not that I was pining for it!) turned into a 'desirable, quirky' coat hanger!

First, get it clean! I know for all I don't like to scrub up spick and span, believing a lick and a spit will surely do, I know it's important for a baby to be clean. So I boiled up some water and mixed it with cold in a washing-up bowl. And got it clean enough. Then – *Make it prettier, brighten it up* – 'tart' is the word they want to use, but don't, being too prissy. So I took the clothes off the baby dolls, the best ones

I could find, and put them on her, even though they were too big, hanging off her in jowls. And, most of all, I gave it some *Tender, loving care*. 'TLC,' Judy says, 'that's all most of these things want. A big helping of TLC, to turn them into something precious!' So I cuddled her, and cwtched her, and sang all the skip songs I could think of. Apples and pears, apples and pears! I like coffee, I like tea, come on baby, cry for me! Clap, clap, clap, clap. And, course, I tried to feed her, though I know well enough it shouldn't be milk from the fridge in an unsterilized doll's bottle, but what else was there? Besides, she didn't want it. Not a drop. Wouldn't even take the teat between her little blue lips. And, day after day, she seemed no better. Never any better. However I tried. Whatever I did. Worse, if anything, which isn't in the Rules. As if I didn't rescue her, after all.

I know the skip's still there, cos I checked last night. It could have been gone – there's rules for that, too. *Be aware – you are only allowed to have the skip for the agreed time limit, after which extra expenditure may be incurred.* There's even still room, if I shift the rotted dog-basket and the tottering tower of 'Good Housekeepings'.

And the baby's quiet – that's good. Not even the faintest of mewling, now.

So it's time to go, being dark again. It's for the best, even though it makes me all empty and cold.

I couldn't give it enough care and attention. That TLC. I see that now. Perhaps the high-heels were right. Perhaps dolls are just plain easier. Or perhaps there just never was any hope. 'Too far gone,' like Judy said about the clock with its workings missing. Like my mother said at the end.

So it's back with it, where it started. A big, metal box full of rubbish thrown away.

You can go to heaven in a little rowing boat. I guess you can go there in a skip, too. I don't see why not.

Lifting Nefertiti

The day before my fiftieth birthday, I decided I wasn't going to grow old any more. I wasn't thinking suicide, or cryogenics, or anything like that. Not even a 'Dorian Gray' portrait, stashed away in an attic I didn't have. Just Egyptian queens or Brazilian Templar snakes. A toss up between the two, really.

At least that's how it started.

What I needed to do was '**defy Time**'. Or so the advert on the Shopping Channel told me. '**Time**' had a capital '**T**', to show how important it was. But I knew that already. Nonetheless, the syrupy, seductive voice of Doctor Sylvester Smythe drooled into my ear 'it will be easy… so EEEZEE!' All I had to do was go to his clinic, take some snake oil, ground dragon's teeth, or unicorn horn, and everything would be fine.

'It's worth a go,' I told my husband – my third husband, Michael, who wasn't actually there. He was hardly there at all by then, but I was still inclined to talk to him. It was Michael who had taught me so much about Time. A Professor of Physics knows such things. When we first met, he would chat about it across the dinner table, over a glass of wine, or as we lay in bed.

'A second is the duration of 9,192,631,770 periods of radiation corresponding to the transition between the two hyperfine levels of the ground state of the caesium atom,' he might say.

Or, 'Terrestrial Time is UT1 = TT – 32.1845 – LS + DUT1.'

Or perhaps it was the other way around…

He taught me even more about it, when he announced he was having an affair with a girl in his department, half my age. They would be moving in together soon, he added. I thought, perhaps, Doctor Sylvester would be able to change all that. If I were younger, perhaps Michael wouldn't need to go. Like James had. And Peter. Like my mother, who had died the year before, in spite of telling me she would never leave me.

My mother was the first person to call me 'beautiful'. She said it from the day I was born. Before, even – cooing 'little princess', 'my prettiest one', as I lay safe, curled in her womb.

She entered me in 'beautiful baby' competitions in every nearby village fete. I always won. Later, it was the carnival Princess, then the Queen. I won all those, as well. She kept a scrapbook full of newspaper cuttings of my successes, and sent them out to various fashion agencies. I suppose that's how I became a 'face' model.

'What other career could you have?' my mother said. She didn't mention they wouldn't want me after thirty.

My first boyfriend kept on telling me I was beautiful, too. They were the first words he said to me, and he said it every single time we went out. Some girls might have found it boring. I didn't. I loved to hear his whispered sweet nothings about how wonderful I looked. They were all I wanted, really. Which was probably why I married him. A mistake.

Michael also said it in the beginning. He'd fallen in love with a photo of me in a magazine. He didn't notice that the mag was ten years out-of-date. It's not unusual for clever men to fall for beautiful women. Think Arthur Miller and Marilyn Monroe. It seems it's rather more unusual for them to stay, though.

'But I've got to try and make him,' I told my mother. I still talked to her, too. Perhaps not as much as before – Michael hadn't liked it when he overheard me.

I told her about Dr Sylvester and what he was offering. 'The service is bespoke, but the snake venom sounds good. It says you can 'TURN BACK THE CLOCK ON AGEING'.'

But I guessed she wasn't the best person to agree with that.

I sent for a brochure from the clinic, and while I was waiting, I decided to research the subject on line. It seemed the sensible thing to do.

'I'm not completely stupid,' I announced to no-one in particular.

Of course, there were hundreds and thousands, or possibly millions, of websites, all '**defying Time**', by offering their own particular elixir of eternal youth.

That's how I found out the snakes weren't Brazilian at all. Doctor Sylvester had got it all wrong. Somewhere along the way, South American killer vipers had got muddled up with their Asian counterparts. Still, I got things straight in the end. The snake I wanted was the Temple Pit Viper. Also known as Wagler's pit viper.

Tropidolaemus wagleri.

Ular Kapuk Tokong.

It lived in Malaysia, in the Temple of Azure Clouds.

'Doesn't that just sound like heaven? Except for the snakes.'

'Well, I suppose that's Paradise for you.' Every now and then, my mother talked back. Which bothered Michael even more.

I phoned the clinic to tell them of their mistake.

'It's the fault of the TV company who produced the ad,' the receptionist declared. 'The equivalent of a typo, you could say.'

And then she told me it wasn't 'snake' at all. 'It's not real venom. Just a herbal imitation of it.'

She began reading from the brochure:

'DDBD blah blah peptide imitating… paralyzing… prey. Postsynaptic membrane… nicotinic acetylcholine receptor…ion canal remains shut. THERE IS NO UPTAKE OF SODIUM IONS!' she finished, triumphantly, as if this were something I should be especially thrilled at.

Next, she began to list all the other things they provided, if I decided against the non-existent snake.

'Body Jet/Fractional Laser Resurfacing/Isolagan/nano-current/meta therapy, lipostripsy/brachioplasty.

Radio Frequency – Pelleve.

Microdermabrasion.

Dermaroller.

Photodynamic Therapy.

Obagi Nu-Derm/Obagi – CR/Obagi Clenziderm/Obagi Elastiderm Eye.'

I began to wonder if she was talking in a foreign language, Brazilian or Egyptian, perhaps. Which reminded me of Nefertiti.

Perhaps the TV people had made a mistake about her, too.

'Oh, no. They got that right. It's definitely Nefertiti.'

At least that was something to be pleased about.

I said I'd think about it and hung up.

'Well… I don't think they can be much good, if they can't get their adverts right,' my mother remarked. 'And what's all this about Nefertiti? What's so special about her?'

Nefertiti was 'the beautiful one' and, once upon a time, a magazine had said I had the same 'look' as her.

'Don't you remember? The long curve of the neck, the chiselled cheek bones, the perfectly arched brows.'

The press-cutting was still somewhere amongst my mother's boxes, filling two of our bedrooms. Something else Michael wasn't happy about.

I knew a lot about the Ancient Egyptians from the Discovery channel, which I liked to watch between Shopping. And I'd seen plenty of documentaries about the Great Royal Wife of Akhenaten, 1376 B.C. She was a favourite subject, because of her looks, fixed for all eternity in a bust by the palace sculptor.

'And somewhere in the desert, they're finding Nefertiti again. It happens all the time. The sand is blown away, a new tomb is revealed, and the archaeologists declare it's her. So there's all this publicity, and money gets thrown. Because that's what beauty can do.

And now it also gets a Botox procedure named after you. 'The Nefertiti lift' because her jaw is so perfect, and the cosmetic powers-that-be have decided age is all in the jaw.'

My hand edged up to my chin. 'No-one would say you're like her any more.' That was me, not my mother.

The last time Michael was here he told me I needed to take a long, hard look at myself. I guessed now was the time to do it. Harsh lighting, no make-up, big mirror – I supposed that's what he meant – so that I could see all there was to see. The skein of lines around my eyes. The brown-age spot on my cheek, that I couldn't pretend was a freckle any more. The red broken veins around my nose. Etc. Etc. Still, make-up could fix all that. It had worked well enough for years. What time took away, Max Factor gave back – or covered over, to be precise. After all, Michael had been fooled by it in the beginning. It had taken him a good while to realize how much older I was than that magazine photo. And by then, it was too late. But my sagging jaw was a different matter.

I decided I'd try the viper potion for my lines, and get the Nefertiti lift for my jaw. It wasn't too drastic. Just a course of needles, costing three hundred pounds, every three or four months. The DDBD I could get from Amazon for a hundred and forty pounds per 30 ml. bottle, so I didn't have to wait for that. It came next day delivery. I started using it at once. Morning, night and in-between, just to be sure.

But really, there wasn't much difference. Michael still said he was leaving.

I found myself wanting 'real'. Surely 'real' was better.

Natural, green, organic, herbal – they never had the punch of the genuine article, no matter what the adverts said. Did vinegar ever get your windows as clean as 'Magic Muscle'? All that jargon the receptionist had given was just a bluff to make you think 'science'. Whereas what you really needed was the snake. Somewhere in the Malaysian jungle I was sure there was an ancient tribe, living on viper venom, who had the skin of new born babies, even when they were a hundred and twenty years old. What was the point of all this 'natural alternative' if it didn't work?

Nefertiti wasn't working, either. Michael came home less and less.

Michael was here, a few weeks ago, fetching the last of his clothes. I told him about the snake poison and Nefertiti lift, so he would know I was making an effort. He looked at me strangely. Perhaps he thought I was talking about an archaeologist getting bitten, while working on the Royal Queen's mummy. It was an easy mistake to make.

'Only… the snake is an imitation peptide and doesn't seem to be much good.'

I told him I thought we needed a holiday. To Malaysia. I could get the real snakes there.

He said he wouldn't be coming back.

Last week, I caught another documentary about Nefertiti, between Shopping programmes. New CT scanning has discovered another bust under the one we all know. There's a bump on her nose, lines on her face, and a not-so-perfect jaw. They think the royal sculptor, Thutmose, had to beautify her with a stucco mask, or get his heart pulled out. Or something like that.

It doesn't matter. People will forget about it quickly. Nefertiti will go back to being the beautiful one. It's easy for her.

I'm climbing up to the Temple now. Reaching towards those clouds, through the azure blue. The snakes inside won't bite me. They've had their fangs cut out, even though the monks deny it all the time. They've even got little red marks on them, to show they've been done. So I'll have to find one in the jungle behind. I'll put out some eggs to entice it to me, then I'll just stand there, until it bites. Two tiny pin-pricks, to make doubly sure. Then the venom will soar through my veins, reaching every part of me, pulling me all together, firming my muscles, lifting my flesh, wiping away my lines. Stopping my blood. Stopping my heart.

And if that doesn't work, I'll go to Egypt, and see if they can make me a plaster mask to cover my head. And if that doesn't fool anyone, I'll ask them to mummify me. They're good at that there. They've had lots of practice. A needle full of embalming fluid – that's all it takes.

After all, I still haven't got my portrait in an attic.
Cryogenics costs two hundred thousand pounds.
But killing yourself is free.

XXX

15 volts… 'It's nothing,' he tells her. 'No more than a tingle, a sensation. 'Oh' is all they say.' Nothing else.

… the same as the current in their NuTone one-touch doorbell. Every evening, she sits there, waiting for the wires to connect, as he presses the button. And when he walks in, he'll stretch up, and kiss her offered cheek. And the harsh bristles of his beard will scrape her lips, scouring through the so-called 'everlasting' Cremesheen of Cherry Dazzle. But that's not his fault. Besides, it's hardly pain. No more than a tingle, a sensation. 'Oh,' is all she says.

She knows about voltages now – volts, ohms, mAs; charges, potentials; how the path of a shock through the body can affect its strength.

'After strenuous exercise, resistance to ground can be reduced to a thousand ohms,' he explained, 'if your feet are bare.'

'Why wouldn't you have shoes on?' she wanted to ask him, but didn't, mustn't. She must pay attention, when he talks about his work, this latest experiment. She must nod and 'mm' in the right places, as if she understands.

15 – the first marker on the machine. Then the slider goes up, the shock goes up.

50 – still no more than an 'oh'.

75 – and, yes, the same. 'Honestly, you'd hardly notice. A shudder, perhaps.'

Until…

90… where the 'oh' turns to more of an 'Argh', then louder, an almost scream.

A slap, she thinks that would be. The kind where the imprint of fingers gets left on a person's cheek. Still, the pain is over quickly, as fast as the ghost-hand fades, so it's not too bad.

It's where it goes from there that really matters.

She's sitting in the hallway, the way he likes her to, waiting for him to come home.

Tonight's going to be okay, though she can never be certain. It's something there's no warning for, not like signs for electric shock hazards. Yellow triangles, with jagged zigzags; children going ZZZ; men with furry outlines jumping in the air. Telling you 'watch out!', 'stay clear!' !!!! Danger. Pain. Death, even.

But no, not tonight.

No need for half-moons scored into her palms, the taste of iron in her mouth ('classic signs of tension', according to the ethics report. The ethics people have been bothering him a lot lately.) But there they are, along with sharp needles sewn into her flesh, the threads stretched tighter towards the moment of his arrival. No need for her 'listening' to go beyond the door, down to the end of the drive, onto the road, as her ears keen for the sound of a Ford engine. She never mistakes it for anything else, not any more. The way the Galaxie purrrrrs along, until the fifth beat, when there's a kind of cough – a clearing of the throat, really. But it's always there. And when she picks up on it, as it moves round the corner of the old Dalton place, she knows she's got one minute fifty-three seconds until the sound of the buzzer.

And that's when the stitches in her stomach loop in and out, and the tangled threads are wrenched towards the door, as if they're surely going to snap, while she holds the shell of her body close, trying to shelter it from harm.

It's the same for the people in Sol's experiment. Only… it's one of the things she hasn't understood, a mistake she keeps on making. The people he's testing are those inflicting the hurt, sliding the shock button up, increasing the voltage; not the ones on the receiving end of it. In other words, it's Sol who should be feeling this terrible tension. And perhaps he is.

That's when she thinks of Eichmann. He stands there, watching the skin-draped skeletons of men, women and children file into the gas vans in Chelmno. 'Whip them,' he says, when they stumble. But what about *inside*? Does he feel it, too – that slight loosening of his bladder, that trickle of warm wetness between his thighs?

Does the bile rise up in his throat and threaten to splutter out between his lips, down onto his proud Iron Cross, second class (or is that because of the smell of the rotting corpses in the forest, before they learnt to bury them deeper?)

And here he is, watching the Jews of Minsk shot in their thousands, falling into the pits, limbs twisted, necks bent, eyes asking something of him. 'My legs felt weak,' he told the court. 'But I had sworn an oath of loyalty. I had been ordered. I had to obey.'

Which is what it's all about. Maybe.

Sol sees Eichmann, too, in his dreams. Every night he lies beside her, moaning, mumbling, until he wakes himself, crying. 'I should have been born earlier, I should have been born over there, not here. I see my grandparents, killed by people who said all they were doing was following orders.'

In the beginning, she felt sorry for him. In the beginning, she comforted him. It seemed the right thing to do.

Please continue.
You must continue.
You have no choice.
You have to do this.

Is this what they said to Eichmann? Eichmann, as he sat in his office, with his figures, charts and percentages, trying to solve the Problem?

It's what they say in Sol's experiment, when the operator doesn't want to increase the shock level, until a man in a grey coat, a 'person in authority' orders him to carry on.

So he does.
90.
100.
110.

One hundred per cent will go as far as three hundred volts. Sixty-five per cent go all the way. No matter what screams they hear, no matter how they beg them to stop. No matter what the pain… except it doesn't exist.

There's no pain, because there are no shocks, the machine isn't real at all. 'Those cries,' he tells her, 'it's a colleague acting a part. They deliberately get things wrong, and pretend the pain is worse. It's to test the operator's obedience to authority, to see if what Eichmann claimed had any validity. I need to know, for my grandparents.'

So it's all a lie, the shocks, the pain, the victims.

But five millions Jews had been killed, hadn't they? And when she raises her fingertip to that little cleft between her cheek and ear, the bone clicks beneath it.

And if what Sol says is true, who is *he* obeying? Where is *his* person in authority?

120 volts.

For a wrong answer, the wrong time and place to be born; the wrong kind of day. Yesterday.

Yesterday, when, for thirty minutes, a crazy, gawky, red-haired female squawked, elbowed and shoved Eichmann and Sol away.

She knows she shouldn't have. She knows days are for housework and 'betterment', not watching re-runs of the 'I love Lucy' show, but she can't help it. Sometimes, she's just got to hear herself laugh – a strange, half-strangled gulp; sometimes she's got to know it can be all right. Sure, Lucy and Ricky fall out now and then, but they always make up by the end. 'They didn't get on for years,' someone told her once. 'They were just waiting for the final series to divorce.' She hadn't believed it, though it turned out to be true. But there's no sign of any discord on the screen, even in this episode, when Lucy gets egg smashed all over her dress, then dances a tango. All they did was laugh, and hug and kiss. Which is all she wants for her and Sol.

But what Sol wants is the best. He doesn't want a wife who didn't have time to do her hair, who spilled sauce down the front of her dress – a small stain, the size of a tear-drop, but far darker than Lucy's sprawled eggs. Who put the oven up far too high, trying to get his dinner cooked in time, and burned it, instead.

120 volts. That's what a cooker is, her top of the range slim-line GEC. Things change around then. That's when it really hurts, so the people being shocked say. 'Hey, this really hurts.' Still, you're not going to die from 120 volts, just like you're not going to die from your head being banged against the wall. Or being yanked to the floor by a handful of your hair, then dragged from the kitchen to the hall, or even when your arm is wrenched behind you, and a fist lands in your stomach, so that you can't breathe. None of that is going to kill you. It's not like having a machine-gun turned on you when you're standing there, with nowhere to run – not that you can run anyway, because your legs don't work, your lungs have no air, from the months of near-starvation, and that journey... Or getting gassed in a van – no escape there, either. It's nothing like that at all.

So… 120 volts. You're not going to die. It's just a lot of pain.

150 volts. 'That's enough.'

165. 'Let me out. My heart's bothering me.'

180 volts. 'I can't stand it any longer.'

270 volts. Screaming, screaming 'let me out of here. Get me out of here. Pleeeaasse!'

'Pleeeease!' It's an easy word to scream. A word you have to open your mouth for. And the eee and the sss are good sounds for stretching out, for yelling through a locked door. A word you hope people will pay attention to. 'You can have/do this, if you say the magic word, 'please'.'

It doesn't work.

It didn't work for the Jews trapped inside those vans, hammering on the doors, crying, begging. A plea – 'please'. Nobody answered, nobody opened the door, Eichmann included.

It didn't work for her the night she was shut in the cellar, a month ago. Well, she guessed no-one could hear her, with their nearest neighbour a half mile away, except for Sol, the one who locked her in there.

She tried all of those things.

She wanted to get out of there, after all. The dark, the cold, the walls getting tighter and tighter, the air getting swallowed up then wasted in her screams. 'Let me out of here/I can't stand it any longer/I can't breathe.' But she could breathe, of course she could – she was lucky. The cellar was around the same size as the gas vans – fifteen feet long, and half as wide – but she was only one person, and there was no gas seeping through a pipe in the floor, so she shouldn't have made a fuss, and beat her fists on the door, or told that little white lie about her heart bothering her, and yet it was nearly breaking. But…

'Please.'

'Please'… it's what she heard him saying to God the next morning, beside the bed, on his knees. Trembling, crying, wringing his hands (all those things the ethics report complained about). Asking for forgiveness, she thought;

begging for help. Until she heard him say, 'Why do you make me do this, Lord?' And then she understood. God was his person in authority. God was telling him what to do.

Eichmann believed in God, too. 'I die believing in God,' were his final words before they executed him. Had God been issuing orders, as well as Hitler, Himmler, and Heydrich? Was that why he couldn't say 'no'?

Prrrr hic, prrrr hic. Ah… she has her one minute fifty three seconds now. But it's going to be all right tonight, she's sure. Except…

…but she's done everything right today. The house is looking like a 'palace', which is what Sol expects. 'Cleanliness is next to godliness,' he says, when he runs his fingers over the furniture, and lifts the rugs to check underneath.

The house in Chelmno was called the Palace; a large, grand manor, with the camp in its grounds. All those jack-boots marching in and out, trailing the mud inside! She doesn't think they'd like mud in there, but they'd fix it soon enough. Cleansing is what they're good at.

… and she is looking perfect, with a bow in her hair, hiding the tender pink patch, pin-pricked with red. And the scarf on her neck hiding the purple stains. And although her arm kinks at the elbow, it's nothing a long, flowing sleeve can't cover.

And the smell of the pot roast (his favourite) says it's just perfect. No, she's done nothing wrong today, nothing wrong at all. Every box has been ticked, no wrong answers. No need for the switch to be raised, the shocks to increase. For 15 to go to 20, 50, 75. No need for God to tell Sol she needs correction. Or for Sol to obey him, like his operators having to obey their instructors' commands, or Eichmann forced to carry out his superiors' orders. No need for them to go through all that anguish. That's right, isn't it? They are the ones in pain – not her, not the Jews, but the ones inflicting the hurt. Not the man attached to the electrodes, channelling the shocks into him (but that wasn't real, was it?). She thinks, she thinks – she's got to get it right, pay attention, and listen to what Sol tells her, she's got to try to understand his work, him… it's what a good wife does. No. Yes. She thinks…

But no, she never knows… that lack of warning signs. Not like in the experiments, when it will always get worse, as the switch gets higher, the voltage increases. And the Jews, there were warnings for them, too, Sol said. 'The burning of the books, Kristallnacht, when the shops and synagogues were destroyed. My grandparents… They knew then, that the Nazis were no friends of theirs. They should have seen what was coming and got out. They should have known.' But they didn't.

She doesn't. Not from the sound of that engine, not from his greeting, which is the same every day. A smile, 'hello darling', and that rough kiss. She had all that yesterday, she will have it today. Until…

15 volts. The doorbell. Fifteen volts. That's all it is.

It wasn't how she thought. It wasn't okay.

300 volts is for thinking wrong. Danger!

340 – the number of corpses that could be burned in twenty-four hours, in Crematorium One, Auschwitz. (Just something that passes through her mind.)

350 – Silence.

400 – Silence.

A silence is worse than a scream, she knows now. Silence was when she was lying there, afterwards.

Silence was the noise in the forest, after all the bodies had been buried.

450 volts. The furthest point, beyond Danger! beyond 'severe shock'. There's nothing more after that, not even a

word. Just XXX.

XXX can mean anything. A string of kisses at the end of a letter, saying ‘I’m going now.’ But would there be kisses then? Even if you still love him?

Or ‘wrong!wrong!wrong!’ Nothing right at all.

Or just the end.

XXX

Goodbye.

Silence.

[W + (D-d)] x TQ/MxNa

[W + (D-d)] x TQ/MxNa

(where W = Weather, d = debt, T = time since Christmas, Q = time since failing our New Year's resolutions, M = low motivation levels, and Na = the feeling of a need to take action).

But D is not defined.

W…

Sleeping, she hears the rain.

'Did you know that dolphins sleep with half their brains awake?' she asked him, once. She thought he would laugh.

Now, she dreams of being a dolphin, racing through the spray, drops of water flying around her face, hitting her firm, lusty flesh. Spit. Spat.

It's the rain, of course, beating on the window, waking the part of her that still dared to sleep. Rain again, rain everyday for the past two months, three weeks, three days. When the curtains are opened, she knows what she will see. Tear-drops working their way down the glass, runnels of moisture blacking next-door's roof. Washed-out grey above, broken only by the shadow-shape of the sycamore. A dome shape. A brain? Her brain, cut open, showing the dendrites that lie there, misfiring, misconnecting, losing themselves, somewhere along the way, shredding, breaking, destroying her sleep. She has seen it like this – they have shown her a diagram, they have taken a scan. They have explained it in hard words, in simple words. So that this is how she sees the bare winter branches of a tree now. This is how she sees everything.

'How can you hear the rain if you're asleep?' he asks her at breakfast.

'Perhaps I am a dolphin.'

She thought he would laugh.

d…

'And this one?'

'Shoes, for the Christmas party. The red heels. You said I should get them.'

'And this?'

'Presents. For your family.'

Why can't he shrug, and say it doesn't matter, it's an expensive time of year? They'll make it up next month, or get a loan, or something. It's only money.

'And *this*? This was only last week!' He stabs his finger at another shop, another number. The lines and curves of letters and figures swim together in front of her, struggling upstream.

'There are other kinds of debt,' she will tell him. 'Sleep, for instance. *A deficit that grows every time you skim extra minutes off your nightly slumber*. Except I skim extra hours.'

Of course, it has all been said before, he has heard it all before, he has seen the scans and the diagrams and the graphs. He is sick of it, she knows.

Instead, she picks up the dishes, and takes them to the sink.

'You said you liked the shoes.' The words drift through her mind, snagging on a loose connection before they reach her mouth. 'Don't do this to me. Please,' she tells the rain.

T…

'… and it's only January 24th!' he shouts after her. 'Another full week till pay-day.' She knows the date – knows it at the start of each morning, when she crosses the day before off the calendar, and fills in her sleep diary, recording how many hours slept (one, two, none), how many hours awake (too many). By lunch time, it will be gone, lost it in the fog-bound morass that surrounds her, along with dolphins and tiny tadpole creatures and things that should be said.

'… a month since Christmas!'

Christmas has been forgotten, too. It has gone in the bin with last year's calendar. It has disappeared amongst those errant dendrites, perhaps, or been weeded out as an unnecessary synapse (*but that only happens during sleep*). She thinks it was nice.

And then he laughs.

Perhaps he finds her dolphin comment funny now! Perhaps he wants to joke about her sleep debt. 'They say it costs America tens of billions dollars. I suppose I shouldn't really grumble!'

And, yes, back at the table, he's reading the paper, instead of punishing his laptop. 'Should have guessed… Blue Monday, the worst day of the year!'

'Of course! There was a feature about it on TV last week.' She had marked it on the calendar with an asterisk. It was good to be prepared. Except she'd forgotten until now.

'Isn't it just nonsense?'

'What else? Just one of those pointless academic equations. Weather… T… Na, something. Psychobabble. Pseudoscience, all done for commercialism. Black Friday. Red whatever. Except it's raining. And that bank statement… The joys of Christmas long gone. Everything downhill from there.'

'Did we enjoy Christmas?' she wants to know.

Q…

He filled a stocking for her. Chocolates, lipstick, tangerines. Earrings, perfume, soap.

Sleep-mask. Earplugs. Kalms. Slipped between the frippery.

The mask is black silk, with lace edging. In another life, she might have worn it in bed for a different reason. (*It's worse if you sleep with someone, you know*).

The earplugs are tiny orange marshmallows. They would float in the coffee that mustn't be drunk. They itch her ears, they fall out. She hears through them, anyway.

She tipped the herbal tablets into the bin. Magic beans. They won't work; she has tried others far more powerful. Benzodiazepine. Zaleplon, zopiclone, zolpiden. ' ZZZ' – some mad scientist having a laugh.

Once upon a time, he told her to take them 'worth a try', meaning 'anything would be better than this!' Until it wasn't.

On New Year's Day, he gave her a list 'so that you won't forget.' 'Just try. New Year, new start!'

Try all those stocking-fillers. (Shut your eyes, your ears, your brain – that's all you have to do.)

Don't sleep in the day/close your eyes if you're tired.

Count sheep. One, two, three… four thousand and ninety-nine.

Exercise more. But not too late.

Eat healthy food. Drink milk, camomile tea. Eat a banana, walnuts, almonds. Have a coffee/don't drink coffee. Chicken/egg; egg/chicken.

'Make a new appointment at the sleep-clinic!' Tie yourself up, plug yourself in, have your head measured, your breathing timed, your brain examined – electro/encephalogram/myogram/oculogram. Have your brain frazzled (no, not that, not quite that!). Just the inside of your brain displayed for all to see. That's why a tree turns into a brain now, why you turn into a dolphin. Or a lab rat. Or Nathaniel Kleitman, who stayed awake for one hundred and fifteen hours. She knows them all, done it all, and nothing works.

'You haven't tried, and it's already January 24th!'

'Why is it 'Q'?' she asks him. But he's already gone.

MxNa…

Chicken/egg; egg/chicken. Don't sleep/get depressed; get depressed/don't sleep.

She will work, now. 'Yes, I will work! I will open my laptop and write that report.' Send it. Brrinngg! It's as easy as that!

Or… 'I will tidy the house.' Yes! Do that first. Start with that, then move on to the work.

Wash the breakfast things.

His mug is still on the table. It sits there, shape-shifting in the fog that hugs her eyes. The marshy soup must be trudged through to reach it. Still, it's in her hand now, safe. Her fingers clench round it, red and white, then unfurl one by one. China petals litter the floor. She looks at them. And looks. And lets them lie.

She'll make the bed. 'That's what I'll do!' It's there, waiting for her, the cover pushed back, asking to be straightened. That's what she came in here for, wasn't it? Or is it asking something else – an invitation, perhaps? 'Come here. Slip between me and the soft, soothing mattress. Let us cocoon you, and cosset you. You can shut your eyes and rest a while. Just a few minutes – a few minutes is alright, just until you feel better. There's nothing wrong in that.'

Tick-tock. Tick-tock. Your heart is fixed to the monitor again. You open your eyes to see the face of the technician beside you. You blink, and blink again, and abracadabra, it turns into the bedside clock, telling you it's gone nine, and he's not home.

You blink some more and see pink elephants, black insects and dwarves clambering up the tendrils of the flowers on the wall-paper. They're nothing new.

Above them, the single eye of the camera, higher than the fog, winks down at you. Only… you're not in the sleep-clinic – remember? But the eye's still there, watching. Watching your every move. Better not to move then. Better to stay where you are, in that in-between space, seeing and unseen; half here, half there. Liminal, they call it. A dolphin again?

Then the one eye turns into two, two slits, glowing like kryptonite, staring. A mouth appears below them, drooling. Drip, drip, drip (just the rain, that's all it is). A shadow crawls down the wall towards you, thickening as it comes.

Gaining weight, because when it's on top of you, you are squeezed, crushed, pushed down, down into the mattress, sinking, drowning. You know who it is. It's not him. It's not him, pressing down on you, into you, making love. That life doesn't happen any more. It's not him, because there's a text saying he's not coming home tonight. He needs some space. Sorry.

You know who it is. The Night Hag. The Ghost, the Mare, the Jinn. You know them all, like you know about dolphins, rats, the giraffe, who sleeps between 0.5 and 4.6 hours, Al Herpin, the man who never slept, Hypnos, the God of Sleep. Hypnosis (risky). Hypno…pompic; hypna… gogic. You've heard about them all; there's nothing you don't know. You know what's happening and why, but still the hands go round your neck, choking your breath away.

Do something. 'You have to do something!' 'Snap out of it! For god's sake!' Enough. Enough. Enough.

MxNa!

So… get up. Push the cover away from you. Swing your legs around, and push your body up. It's not so hard, is it? Put your clothes on – oh, they're on already – just your shoes then. The red ones, perhaps. Why not? And your coat. Put a few magic beans in the pocket. Pop a few in your mouth, first. And walk out of the door.

D…

It's quiet here, by the water. No-one else is about. Even the ducks are peaceful, tucked away into the bank for the night. 'Did you know that the ducks at the front and back of the line will keep one eye open to sleep?' she told him once. Or twice. Or three times. 'Not so different from dolphins, really.' She guesses he was fed up of dolphins a long time ago. 'Perhaps I should have told him about Rechtschaffen's rats, instead.' They whirl in front of her now, clinging to their spinning disc, round and round and round, forced to stay awake, or be thrown into the water. After two weeks, they were all dead. 'From exhaustion… nothing else.'

Perhaps she did tell him. 'I thought rats could swim,' he said. 'Nowhere to swim to, in a tank in the lab.' Perhaps he laughed.

She pictures dozens of them clutching each other, crying, (do rats cry?); sees their eyelids sinking, their desperate limbs sliding until… splash! Awake, again, always awake.

She could be one of them now, standing here with water all around her, except she is alone. She pictures him beside her, clutching her, crying. 'We are skimming extra minutes off our love,' he will say, 'with each word said or unsaid, with each look, or ignoring.' 'Debt is what we owe each other. Love is a debt,' she will reply. But he isn't there.

She walks into the water. Gentle waves break around her feet. Theta waves, delta waves, any which waves, lapping against her, soothing her. She will close her eyes for a moment and rest, just rest…

D is for…

Whale Watching

She was standing on the headland when the whale came into view. Dishrag white, a floating giant barnacle. The man was spread cross-like on its flank, caught in a cat's cradle of harpoon hemp. There was no-one else to see it, only her. She had started running as soon as it left the harbour; she knew the way. The creature turned towards her, watching her from its one pig-eye; the man looked, too. And then it turned again, facing the open sea.

The man waved to her, as they disappeared into the mist, towards Ireland.

'Goodbye,' she said, waving back.

When she told, toothless gums nah-nahed at her, hands came together and trapped her in a corner of the school-yard. Names boxed her ears.

'Thicko!'

'Fibber!'

'Twpsin!'

'Liar, liar…'

And yes, next day, at the harbour, the whale was there again, and the waving man was walking about, talking to the crowd.

'There!' her teacher told her. 'You mustn't make things up! That's what films are for!'

'Miss' spent her Saturdays at the Palace in the big town. 'We must visit the set as often as we can,' she told the school. 'It will be an educational experience.' She brought *movie* magazines into class, and showed them pictures of the *stars*. One day, she brought the book, which had the same name as the film. 'It's too old for all of you, but I shall read you some.'

'Call me Ishmael,' she began. It was enough.

She told them how brave the whale-hunters were, how many useful things came from whales.

They lived in Wales, didn't they? The children scratched their heads.

'Margarine. So much better than butter, so much easier for cooking! Oil. Potions for your mothers' lotions and make-up. Where would we be without them?'

They made models out of newspaper, water and flour. The boys put them in puddles and watched them sink.

Whenever they visited Lower Town, where the filming took place, teacher's legs grew longer and shinier. Her lips were red against pale, pillowed cheeks, beneath coils of hair, stacked like lobster-pots. She edged the children towards the stars, careless of the water, the *lens* of the camera. The *director* motioned them away, the teacher's cheeks reddened, even through their whale-oil glaze. Yet they still went back the next day.

Weeks later, after the film crew had gone, and the coast was quiet once more, she climbed to the headland again. Far below, pieces of rotting carcass were washed along the shore; caught amongst the jagged outcrops, floating in the rock pools, along with a pink hair-slide. Later still, she saw a group of seals playing with scraps of white flesh, passing them from nose to nose, smiling.

And there was blood, she was certain there was blood… spreading strands like dulse seaweed – on the seals, on the rocks. How could there be blood if it wasn't real?

She knew what she had seen, and if she had seen it, it must be true.

Soon, the people of the town forgot, going back to their fishing and farming; waiting for holiday-makers who never came. In time, another film came along, with new actors. Brighter stars in even bigger cars, who stayed longer; who were Welsh, like them, and drank in the pub, rather than the big hotel; drank in the pub again and again. Other things were different, too. Cameras taking photos of cameras, televisions in every house, some of them in colour. (Marriage.) Phones in every house, to make gossiping easier; cars in every drive, making the world smaller. (Children.) Soon the old film was forgotten. Only she remembered. Remembering, as she dredged nappies through bleach-water, her hands as wizened as the whale. As her husband snored beside her. As she wrote her name in the dust on the shelf, where the book lay. She had bought it she didn't know when… or perhaps when the librarian told her one too many times 'you've borrowed this before!'

A heavy book, as heavy as the creature, full of weighty words, that she couldn't understand, meanings she could never fathom. The Whale meant something. The Hunt meant something. But what? And the teacher had lied when she said it began with 'Call me Ishmael'. Page after page must be got through before that, lines, paragraphs speaking of Leviathans, and Spermacetti, and Rights and Orks. How they killed, or were killed. Of their bones and teeth decorating the land.

There was no Great White, the white came later, in the story proper. She drew the book out, from where it stood, amongst thinner, lighter tales of nurses and doctors in love, or Cowboys fighting Indians. She wanted to read it, but the alien words floundered in her head, 'hypos/Manhattoes/circumambulate' flailing against the children's crying and squabbling, and her husband's complaining. She put it back in its place.

And soon it didn't matter that she couldn't read it. The film came back to her, in a little plastic box she must post beneath the television. She could watch it again and again, while the family yakked and pulled and grew around her. All she had to do was press a button, and rewind.

When the famous actor died, the local paper printed his picture, writing about his visit to their little town. Scrunching her eyes over her glasses, the points of her scissors laboured around the article, with her thickened knuckles, her stiff thumb. She put the piece in her special box, with all her other cuttings, yellowed by the years.

'I met him,' she told anyone who would listen. 'He put his hand on my head, tangling my hair.' She was afraid for her new pink slide. Her mother had rowed her for losing the old one on the cliffs. The day she had seen the whale.

'Call me Ahab,' he said, his voice dragging his words, low. There was something wrong about that... If he was Ahab, there would be only one long black pleated leg facing her. There would be a white line cloven down his face. He wouldn't smile, which he did, before moving back through the crowd.

Later, he appeared on the step of the trailer, his cheek forked like lightning. His wooden leg caught between the treads. She was glad. It made sense again.

'The whale bit it off at the knee,' someone in the crowd whispered. 'It's not wood,' another voice added. 'It's the bone of a whale.'

'It's not bone… it's…'

Whatever it was, *he* was as he should be… if he was Ahab. Until he smiled at her again.

Her teacher shot slit-eyes at her and pulled her away.

'I know, now, that it was jealousy. I didn't understand then.' Perhaps she should have left her story there. But no, the words spilled out of her mouth, bubbling up, as she told how she had seen the whale, far out to sea, with the actor strapped to its side.

There was no name-calling any more, but faces turned away, hands lifted to stop sniggering breath. People in the market, her children. Not her husband; he, too, was dead by then.

'You're muddling what you think you saw with the ending of the film,' Mari, her daughter, told her.

How did *she* know? She hadn't been born then; she

herself was only a child, a small child. Had she ever seen the film? 'Only a million times, when we were growing up!'

'Look!' she said to no-one in particular; Mari, who had already walked away, her dead husband, an empty room, showing them another photo from her box, one she had cut from a film magazine, when her fingers moved more easily. 'There! That's me!'

And it was; a girl, of about five, with her fringe pulled back by a slide; pink, it would be if there was colour. A girl with a Peter Pan collar, and Mary Jane shoes. A pleated skirt, with a pin in it. She was standing at the front of the crowd, on the edge of the quay. That was the first day of filming, before the visits with school.

Her fisherman grandfather had gone there early, hearing they may want him – or his boat – and he had taken her. So she was there, at the very beginning, when the big, shiny cars arrived, when the ship with its three tall masts pulled into the harbour, when the hammering, shouting, dragging, lifting started, to make towers of wood for the cameras, to hide fronts of houses, to make new ones, which were old.

'See,' her grandfather said. 'Those ships are just the kind that would have berthed here last century. See, that car... you'll never see a tidier one round here.' Time chopped and churned with the tide, in front of her eyes.

'I went every day after that. Early, before school. Late, after. And then there were our visits with the teacher. That's how I'm in the photo. I was there so much, always near the front.'

That's how she was so quick to spot the whale heading out to sea. Why she was the first to run. Why only she saw it.

Time was like that now, rewinding, fast-forwarding like her video tapes. Soon, there were grandchildren to tell, to show the yellow pages. When they were small, they nodded and smiled, and said 'yes, how wonderful, Nain.' She hugged them and their words close. She put them in a different box.

But they grew, too.

'Tell us about Taid, Nain,' they would say. 'Shall we look at some photos of him?' Perhaps there were some, somewhere, but she didn't know where, and her film box was always at hand.

One of them, his name just beyond reach, took the faded picture from her, looked at it near his eyes.

'This isn't here, Nain. It's in Ireland. See the signs in the street behind? And our harbour has the cliff rising above it. That can't be you.'

She looked at the picture again. The boy didn't know how the film men could change things, how they could change young men into old, and back again, legs into ivory stumps, rubbish bins into barrels, how they could paint a cliff in, or take one away.

It was her. She had been there.

The grandchildren came with the summer, sent for sun and fresh sea air. Yet they spent their days staring at screens, and flicked their thumbs up and down. They said you could find the whole world in a phone.

Still, if she asked, they would take her to the harbour. There was colour, now. Blue, red, yellow painted houses. An ice-cream van. Rainbow sun-shades.

'Much better,' people said.

The film people had taken the colour away – what little there was back then. They didn't want it. Not here. They wanted drab stone, moulding wood, grimed window-panes. Cobbles. They could magic all these, as they had done with the cliff, and the signs. But it had been many years before the colour came, following the tourists, who had finally discovered the town, along with their ice-creams and crab sandwiches and boat-trips. Yes, they did that now, sleek, fast boats, out into the bay; bird-watching, dolphin-spotting, paying good money. 'No sightings guaranteed…' When they came back, she would hear their wonder. 'I saw a fin!'

'It jumped out of the water!' 'They followed us for ages!' A whale, sometimes, a small affair, and yet they made such a fuss.

What was so special about this, she asked herself? Dark curves, that could hardly be glimpsed, except through a glass. Camouflaged by the black troughs of the sea, except for those showy jumps.

Her whale moved on top of the water.

It was white, and huge.

'I've seen a whale,' she wanted to say, the words coming close to her mouth.

'I've seen a whale,' she said. 'Here, just here, and then…'

The children, or children's children, hurried her away.

On her good days, they would take her to the cliffs, where the farm had been.

'I was born here, it was my home,' she would tell them, waving towards the buildings behind her. Holiday cottages, now, 'sought after, in sight of the sea.' Yes, it was what she woke up to, every day. It was part of her. They had said the same about the story; the sea was part of it, too. The sea meant something, like those other things that were supposed to mean something.

This place, high up, looking both ways, was one of her favourites. The water did everything here, on different days, at different times. And it was where she had seen the whale disappear.

'I ran, as soon as the mooring broke free. I knew which way it would go; I knew the currents. They – the film people – followed only the marked tracks, and stumbled at each outcrop. Have I told you this before?'

She followed the beast along the coast, running from cove to cove, over the cliff tops.

'My pink hair-slide broke free and skittered down the cliff. I couldn't see above the height of the gorse, but I knew where I was going – home. I was the one who got here first.

I was the one to see the whale rounding the corner. I was the one to see it disappear, with the famous actor tied to the side.'

They always shuffled glances then, in time with their feet; their thumbs would start that fidgeting again, and they would say 'No, no!' 'It wasn't like that at all.' 'Look, it says here…'

They showed her things she didn't want to see – a picture of a white cylinder, with wires and cogs behind, a man pulling levers inside.

'Look!' They were fond of that word. And she lowered her eyes to whatever was on the little screen. But she saw nothing, she didn't have to see, unless she wanted to.

They told her things she didn't want to hear.

There was no whole whale. Just bits – a tail, a head, sections that they moved around on a barge, putting them in the water when needed. Or… there were three models, but none of them whole…

Sixty feet, eighty-five feet, one whale, three. No whales, parts of whales, a model in a tank; a picture on a studio wall. Rubber; steel.

'An internal engine to pump the spouting water!'

'Dye in the latex skin, so that it could 'bleed'!'

'A publicity stunt, Nain! Just imagine the press coverage such a story would get. 'Hollywood star nearly drowns, swept out to sea on the back of a whale!''

'A myth,' another announced. 'Built from half-truths, a muddle of events. Look, a section broke free; the actor nearly drowned being dunked in a tank in the studio. Then they all said different things. The coastguard sailed to the rescue! The R.A.F. was called! But none of it happened! The camera guy says this… the director says that… Gregory Peck something else entirely! But they all seem to settle on 'no whale!''

'No,' she said. 'They must have forgotten. They had so much to do. They moved on quickly.'

They moved on to another film, another story. It became nothing to them.

The children leave with the summer. She is glad.

Soon, everything they've said is gone again. All the 'looks' bundled away, along with their forgotten names. And the whale drifts out of the harbour, great, white, whole, with the famous actor trapped in a web of twine. She runs along the cliff, her pink slide falls, and there it is again.

Soon, she sees the sea every day, just as in her childhood, in this place they've put her in, calling it 'home'. Home again, sea again.

And there are new people who listen to her story, and say 'How interesting!' Or, 'Good!' no matter how many times she tells. She cannot see the film anymore – her eyes are too dim. Besides, none of the other 'residents' want to watch it. But the nice girls will read to her from the book, if she asks, when they have the time.

It is the ending she wants to hear. How Ahab raises his hand from the flank of the whale, beckoning his crew to carry on with the kill.

'I saw it,' she tells them. 'I saw the whale disappear into the mist, with the famous actor tied to its side. He waved at me, so I said 'Goodbye.''

'No,' the girl who is reading to her that day, tells her; a girl who pays attention to the words on the page. 'Ahab gets pulled into the water. It's the Parsee who is caught on the whale. And he doesn't wave. They changed it for the film. They changed the whole ending. It's what they do, for dramatic effect.'

After the girl has gone, she puts the book in the bin.

And the whale turns towards the open sea, and the man raises his hand to her.

'Goodbye.'

Trouble Crossing the Bridge

'Soon, I will be falling. Not the crumpled collapse of a Woolworth pocket-money toy; nor the glairy smasshh! of a nursery-rhyme egg. But the languorous, somersaulting descent of the angel-boy, who foolishly flew too close to the sun. Or just down, down, down.'

This is what she's supposed to say, what he wants to hear – call-me-Joe, in his granny-knit cardigan, who sits opposite her, holding her life in a brown manila folder. And then he will save her, reach out his arm and save her from the troll who hides under the bridge, waiting for her to fall.

Instead, Lena's telling him about the toy. The story slips down the synapses of her brain, trips off her tongue, as easy as once-upon-a-time.

'A wooden cat, found in the bottom of my Christmas stocking, along with a mouldering tangerine and a handful of nuts! A cat on a drum, hiding a button beneath. 'You have to press there,' Ellie told me, snatching it away.'

And the cat, proud, poised and taut, as any Egyptian god, fell helplessly down, until her sister let go, springing it back up. They both laughed. 'My turn, my turn!' she, Lena, cried. Then it was up/down, up/down, until her thumb faltered, and Ella grew bored and wandered away. Later, 'I saw how fine lengths of thread passed through its hollow limbs. I snipped each one with my mother's sewing scissors.' The cat fell apart for good.

She likes to tell about the cat; it's something she told all the others – all the other kindly listeners, desperate for something to add to her file. File/Life – she likes that, too. A mistake, though, to tell about the scissors, perhaps.

And she tells him about Humpty Dumpty. Why not? And all those other precarious nursery-rhyme characters. The Grand Old Duke, Jack and Jill, all climbing or tumbling, unable or unwilling to be happy on flat, solid, ground. These were the ones her mother favoured – no sweet baa-lambs, or garden girls for her. Still, it was something; the only thing. Her mother's single effort at entertaining her daughters, reciting the verses over and over, as if simple rhyming repetition was all she could manage. No mimicry, no performance – just a clenched grin forcing out each laboured syllable between her teeth. Had-A-Great-Fall.

It was left to her father to weave the words of winding fairy-stories into her ear, binding her with their spells. To take her on his lap, and tell her enchanting tales of distant lands, where magic carpets flew through the air, along with boys with waxen wings, and white horses with golden horns – 'Whooshhh! Swisshh! Abracadabra!' There were stories from her own land, too, where genies turned into witches, Ali-babas into fairies, Argonauts into Arthur's knights. And the minotaur/giant/Cyclops became the troll, who jumped out from behind cupboards, curtains and doors, arms swinging, fol-di-rol-ing/I'm a Troll-ing.

'In the beginning…' In the beginning, she and her sister would squeal with delight and run away to their rooms. That was in the beginning. But soon the tales grew dark. And he must tuck her up in bed, then move in beside her to tell them. Succubae and incubi able to tease their way through unseen crevices in window frames. 'Behind the curtain! Put your hand there, and feel the draught!' Ghosts able to sidle through stone walls, daubed with mud, lathe and horse-hair, two feet deep. 'But somehow they can. There!' She had thought the night-time sound scratching at her ears was no more than spiders rummaging through the plaster. But no. 'They do things to you. The monsters come into your room in the dark and do things to you.' She knew that; she had seen them. Or one at least. It had the face of the troll.

Don't tell. Something bad will happen if you tell. Besides, no-one will believe you. Don't tell, ever. EVER.

She knows she should tell call-me-Joe about the Troll, as he crinkles his face at her, makes clucking noises, and cleans his square, black spectacles, with the hem of his cardigan. 'Wool is no good for that,' she wants to tell him. Just as she wants to tell him about the Troll, she really does. He is kind. He deserves to know. And it is what he wants to hear – not about a falling cat, or childish rhymes, with their da-de-das/la-la-las. And she knows, if she tells him, that he may see things differently, and not talk to her of bridges inside her head.

'The problem is *there*,' he tells her, as he pulls books pell-mell from the shelf behind him, spreading a ream of brains onto the desk between them. Spongy corrugated grey matter magicked into daubs of rainbow colours; a microscopic journey into a forest of trees, branches, twigs. A slice of brain transformed into a series of blocks and lines...more ups and downs, more greens, blues, reds. And here is one like hers, opened out and pushed towards her, a hemisphere on each side. '*There*' is a filament lost between the fold of the page, lost between the two halves of her mind. Lost in long Latin words and medical jargon. So, 'Bridge is easier,' he says. 'Think of it as if something is stopping traffic crossing over a bridge.'

'That may be why you hear things, see things.'

Or maybe not.

She will need to enter the white tunnel now. To lie there, unmoving, filling her mind with its sound. 'We can be sure then,' he says. 'The corpus callosum will show up on the image.' Amygdala/orbitofrontal/medial cerebral' – another rhyme to play through her head.

Yet of course, he was right, there was a bridge. It was where trolls lived, after all, when they weren't jumping out from cupboards, or creeping into your room. ('Under the rickety bridge,' her father had sung to her. 'He'll eat you for supper!' he had screeched.) They hid under the arches, lost in the shadows, waiting for unwary travellers to pass by. Or just those they knew.

She could see this real bridge clearly, where it lay no more than a giant's spitting distance from their home, reaching across the river. She knew it well – she and her sister had had to cross it every day to get to school. A high bridge. High was what mattered.

'There's a place…' she tells Joe now. Perhaps if she gives him this, he will not turn her mind into a picture, to be pored over, twisted into words and slotted into the file. '…beside the water. There are trees on the bank, with the mountains behind. A place where…'. Say it, say it, but she can't. A slip in those synapses, a trip in her tongue? Or just **You see! That's what happens when you tell! I told you something bad would happen. It's your fault. Remember! So don't tell again!**

'Yes!' Joe's voice jumps in, between her thoughts and words/his thoughts and words, triumphant. 'There are often places where the voices are heard more clearly, the imagined echoing the real. Sometimes, it helps to revisit and absorb them, and accept them for what they are.'

Maybe. Perhaps. Or maybe not.

Still, here she is, doing what she was told, like a good girl, as she'd always been, until… Back where she has never been 'back' before, sitting on a bench above the river, waiting for the voice to come.

She had arrived early, with the sun just rising. She wanted it to be quiet, so that she could hear better. ('All the better to hear you with' – another of the tales he had spun; another one he liked to act out. He was the wolf, of course. Under the bedclothes). Behind her are the mountains, where they had lived, along with the giants, and all the other treacherous creatures. Ahead is Life/File – one or other; or neither. All she has to do is cross the bridge to get to whatever it is going to be. Eeny-meeny, minny, mo – another game they had played. Ella/Lena, Lena/Ella, until Ella was too old for such things.

And now she hears him, singing in her handbag, demanding to speak to her in no more than a hundred and forty characters. Somewhere down below her are the arches, where the voice should be coming from, where the troll should be living. The children's bogey-man, long-haired, goggle-eyed and long-armed. But the shadows are empty.

Trolls are different now. You find them in different places. They follow you on the magic web, creeping unseen into your life, along endless lengths of fibres. Into your home. Into your phone. That's where he is now, chirping like a bird. That's what he's been doing, ever since he returned.

Golden Gate, Humber, Clifton Suspension.
Sydney Harbour, Bosphorus, Tuira.
Nanjing Yangtze River. Sunshine Skyway…

Sunshine Skyway – as if, going up, you could reach the brightest star, while 'down' spelled certain doom. Wasn't that the fate of the angel-boy in the tales from far-away lands, from long, long ago? Wasn't that the fate of…

Two hundred and forty-five feet above the flower city's harbour.

Four seconds to hit the water, at seventy-five miles an hour.

So the boy's descent hadn't been slow, after all! And there had been no gentle welcoming by the sea, no waves waiting to open their arms and gather him close, as she had liked to imagine. As she had wanted to believe.

Twelve hundred and eighteen before they stopped counting.

The first just ten weeks after its opening.

Ten in a month, the highest tally.

All those lives lost, all those broken people…

…broken by the fall, limbs, necks fractured,
Organs ruptured.
Crack. Smashhh!

And there she is, in the water beneath Lena, who is standing now, half way across the bridge. Her mother, waving up to her. And there she is, disappearing beneath the surface, down, then up again, then down, then up, like the foolish toy, or the Duke's ten thousand men. Until she doesn't come up any more.

And there she is, on the bank, tendrils of weeds for her hair, her eyes empty. Her neck twisted one way, her leg straight out from her body.

No!

Yes! Had-a-great-Fall!

'Shut up! Shut up!'

Black and blue, streaked with red, her head crushed like her pathetic nursery-rhyme egg. Her bones as dislocated as that cat!

Shut up, shut up, shut up!

Like you didn't do! I told you not to tell. I told you. But

you did, didn't you? You told her. And look what happened next!

Lena takes a step forward towards the edge. She feels the words wind themselves around her, just as they used to do, pulling her further, out into the breeze.

Come on, come on, you can do it. Another step, then another. And then you'll be back with her.

She takes another step. Gaping mouths sweep past her in car windows, without stopping.

Barriers built, to try and save them.
One hundred and eighteen talked down by do-gooders.
But where's the fun in that?

She is Humpty Dumpty, struggling to stay on his wall. She is Jill, poised between tumbling after Jack, or keeping to the safe, straight path. She is her mother, knowing her daughter is telling the truth, clutching her arms to her sides and swaying back and fore, until Lena is sure she will fall to the floor. She is her mother standing where Lena is standing now, unable to stay on firm solid ground any longer.

Don't disobey, like the angel-boy! He should have listened to his father! You should have listened to your father. Listen now!

No!

Yes! Hurry, come on, think of it as flying! Jump!
Flee! Fly! Fo! Fum! Remember that one?

And yes, she would like to fly, fly free like the birds.

'Did you know that birds are like the Woolworths' cat?' she wanted to tell Joe. 'They have air cavities in their bones. Pneumatisation, it is called.' But she was afraid of another black mark in the file.

Ella had flown, too. A different kind of flight, in a big white bird to another land.

And then her father, running away from the questions that would be asked, after her mother had leapt into the sky.

Until the day her phone had rung, and the bird had sung. Tweet, tweet, tweet.

Joe doesn't know. The white tunnel doesn't show such things. Talking doesn't tell such things, if you don't say. So it's not his fault he thinks there's something wrong with her brain. It's not his fault that he thinks it, along with her personality, are split in two. And yet, 'You don't have to listen to the voices,' he told her, when she said she would visit the bridge. 'No matter how strong, no matter how insistent. You don't have to listen at all!'

Eeny, meeny, minny, mo…

Eeeny, meeny, troll or Joe.

Lena takes the phone and throws it high into the air. Up, up towards the sun. Then down it comes, somersaulting, down, down, down. A languorous descent.

She walks on across the bridge.

Acknowledgements.

Some of these stories first appeared in the following magazines and anthologies: The Lonely Crowd ('Herr Munch Visits the Zoo'); The Blue Nib ('The Cabinet of Immortal Wonders' and 'The Woman who Never Begs'); Leicester Writes Short Story Prize Anthology 2018, by Dahlia Publishing ('XXX'); Ruins – an anthology, by Cinnamon Press ('[W + (D-d)] x TQ/MxNa'); Crannog ('Trouble Crossing the Bridge').
'Whale Watching' won first prize in the 2019 ChipLit Festival Competition, and is due to be published in Salt's Best (British) Short Stories 2020. [W + (D-d)] x TQ/MxNa was a runner-up in the 2016 Cinnamon Short Fiction Award, and subsequently appeared in Ruins, the winners' anthology.
Thanks to those editors and judges.
And to family and friends, as ever.
Many thanks to David Powell (my husband!) for his wonderful photography and design for the cover.

And particular gratitude to the editors at Chaffinch Press for making this happen.

Printed in Poland
by Amazon Fulfillment
Poland Sp. z o.o., Wrocław